BRUSHSTROKES FROM THE PAST

A HISTORICAL ART MYSTERY

A SOLI HANSEN MYSTERY: BOOK 4

HEIDI ELJARBO

Editor: Jill Noelle Noble

Cover Design: Tim Barber, Dissect Designs

Layout: Linn Tesli

Visit https://www.heidieljarbo.com/ to read more about her books, news, events, and you can sign up for e-newsletters to hear about new releases.

PRAISE FOR HEIDI ELJARBO'S

SOLI HANSEN MYSTERIES

"Superbly written: A thrilling and suspenseful combination of art and the Resistance that kept me riveted until the very last page."
-USA TODAY Bestselling Author, Kathryn Gauci

"The two timelines inform each other beautifully...all described in sumptuous detail. If you love the art world and a good mystery, you will really enjoy this well-written book which has plenty of excitement and intrigue to keep you turning the pages...a highlight for me in descriptive writing." *-Deborah Swift, historical novelist*

"A fresh and compelling read! From front to back cover churns a nonstop, multi-layered plot weaving post-war street savvy with high Italian art; espionage with friendship; murder with survival ... all through artful prose and at a pace that makes for a can't-put-down, first-class literary voyage." *-Melissa Dalton-Bradford, author*

"This richly detailed, perfectly paced mystery effortlessly weaves together art history, narrative, and the palpable fear of working undercover. Soli continues her personal growth, emerging as a confident heroine who is willing to risk it all to save the paintings she loves."
-Lynn Morrison, author

"How quickly this story and characters captured my interest. This author is one to watch!" *-Christina Boyd, author*

"With a visceral understanding of the audience this story is intended for, Heidi Eljarbo has once again presented her readers with a book that has not only been meticulously researched but also one where the narrative is so utterly enthralling that I lost all sense of time...
This series keeps getting better and better. It is so tantalisingly brilliant that each page becomes a voyage of discovery...fabulous from beginning to end. This series deserves a place on your bookshelf and in your heart."
-Mary Anne Yarde, The Coffee Pot Book Club

"Absolutely incredible!" -Passages to the Past

"The overarching theme of finding (and fighting for) light in times of darkness was a great backdrop for this novel that skillfully juxtaposes good and evil like a chiaroscuro painting." -Bruce Jacobs, author

"Alongside this fast-paced, energetic story is the story of the origins of the painting, so we also spend some time in the seventeenth century. It is all very Dan Brown!"
-OhLook,AnotherBook

"Artfully told historical mystery... You'll have to read Eljarbo's entertaining book to find out."
-The Historical Novel Society

"The setting and characters were extremely well written and believable. Suspense, and mystery, and romance, and all the good things are all rolled up together to make a great book." -Tifani Clark, author

BOOKS BY HEIDI ELJARBO

Courageous Clara Dahl:
Catching a Witch
Trailing the Hunter

Soli Hansen Mysteries:
Of Darkness and Light
The Other Cipher
Hidden Masterpiece
Brushstrokes from the Past

Heartwarming Christmas:
Fair Mountain Christmas

Mysteries of the Modern Ladies' Society:
Secrets of Rosenli Manor

For Sean.

You are brave, kind, and one who protects.
I cherish your hugs, and I am eternally grateful to call you my son.

*I bury my head in the pillow, and dream of my
true love…
I am rowing to you on the great, dark ocean.*

Amor Vincit Omnia
(Love conquers all).

— CARAVAGGIO

CAPITOLO I

VESTFOLD, NORWAY LATE AUGUST 1641

WOLFERT DID NOT want to admit he was at death's door. He never thought of dying as a romantic notion but rather a cruel way to drag him from the life he knew. For he cherished his life, a good meal, and laughing with trusted friends. Too often, he'd overheard soldiers on the battlefield stating an act of fearlessness, something to leave as a legacy of their heroism. But Wolfert was not interested in such outward boldness. He was merely trying to get through the days. If only he had a priest walking alongside him now, one who could steer his thoughts to loftier places and make his journey north less brooding...a priest to remind him of heavenly peace and cherubs playing soothing music on golden harps.

He stopped to stretch his back on a route through the beech forest and turned to scan the area behind him to make certain no one followed. How his whole body cried with pain. What had started as a small scrape to his skin had become an infection-ridden menace. He had himself to blame. First, because he'd picked a fight. Second, because he'd ignored the ever-festering wound and had not taken the time to find an ointment or healing balm. Had he been more watchful, the small cut would not have swelled into a horrid gash. Adjusting the dressing across his breastbone caused him to groan in agony. Only stubbornness kept him going. Shivering with cold, he pushed his hair back under his blue hat and continued along the winding path. Tall spruce and pine trees dotted the woodland up ahead. Yestereve, midnight had come with a starlit sky, but as the morning approached, the early song of birds had diminished, and fog had blurred the trail like an unfinished painting.

He was well acquainted with art. One could say he was a connoisseur—he'd even apprenticed with the great Rembrandt for a season. But Wolfert's talents and interests lay elsewhere. After stealing his first piece of artwork as a youngster, he'd discovered a way to make money much faster than by wiping a brush back and forth on a canvas. His admiration for the old master painter was deep. It just wasn't a profession for him.

Once he returned to Amsterdam, things would change. He'd be a well-heeled man with the means to rent a proper townhouse and could finally build up enough courage to ask the fair Catharina to marry him. It was time to settle down with a good woman by his side, have half a dozen children, and find a more respectable profession.

How long until he reached the main road? Wolfert had sold stolen art in the area thrice before, but then, his body had been strong, not filled with throbbing aches tearing at every limb. Several wealthy men of influence showed interest in his wares. Most of them lived in the capital Christiania. This time, the buyer was a nobleman and an avid art collector who had his residence in the country a little farther south. Most importantly, the nobleman never asked where the artwork came from, only cared that each piece was exceptional, authentic work in good condition.

Wolfert adjusted the rope on his shoulder and pushed the wooden tube he carried on his right hip. The wound to his flesh across his lower ribcage was not his major concern now. He had to reach the buyer's residence by nightfall. First the transaction, then he'd pay a visit to a physician. Excruciating pain told him this was far worse than any bruises or injuries he'd gained previously in tavern brawls and battles. This wound would not heal without proper help. Oh, why had he picked a fight with a musketeer? The Frenchman was in King Louis XIII's guard, for mercy's sake. There was nothing wrong with Wolfert's strength and experience, but Claude Beaulieu had, unfortunately, been better trained.

Then there was the Frenchman's wife. Wolfert had never thought he'd see the day when a beautiful woman could handle the sword like a musketeer. What was the world coming to?

Slanting rain pierced through the treetops and wet the ground. Where could he find shelter? If he were to lie down under a thick spruce, he might fall asleep. In an open clearing farther up the path, he noticed a rocky hill on the other side of a marsh. A small cave would be better. He could light a fire, roast the rabbit hanging from his belt, and rest for a moment before he continued. Howling sounds from a lone wolf sounded in the distance. Or was it alone? Had it caught his human scent? The animal wouldn't care if it had a namesake, a poor, two-legged struggling to make it to his destination. Wolfert marched forward through the swampy wetland, trying to step on more solid spots, stumbling now and then. Hopefully, the old gray wasn't hungry enough to be interested in seeking him.

Slowly moving across the bog, Wolfert imagined sitting in front of a warm fire with the lovely Catharina, drinking wine from crystal goblets. Lulled in his own thoughts, it seemed as if the world around him ceased to exist. As his body hit the ground beneath him, Wolfert fell into oblivion, and everything went dark.

WEDNESDAY, 25 APRIL 1945

CHAPTER ONE

VESTFOLD, NORWAY

ONLY A FEW PATCHES of snow were left in the shadiest parts of the forest. A lazy haze drifted horizontally between the tall trunks of pine, slowly lifting before melting into the rays of the early morning sun.

"How much farther?" Soli asked.

"From the map, I'd say five or ten minutes." Heddy opened the lid of the tin box containing cold, boiled potatoes and herring. "Do you want some more?"

Soli picked up another piece of fish, put it into her mouth, and licked her fingers. Her mind raced with curiosity. An old archaeologist had contacted her by messenger boy the evening before. Professor Holst had been a respected member of the university faculty in Oslo for decades. Even after the Germans shut down the institution of higher education in the capital, they'd allowed him to continue teaching under the direction of *Nasjonal Samling*, the only legal political party during the war. Perhaps they thought he'd discover something of great value, treasures they could take back to their notorious Führer. But the desire to freely learn could not be stopped. The Illegal Academy for artists had been established in 1941, and their administration kept the professor's extracurricular supervision in the dark. Art students secretly received their education in a loft above the corset manufactory—called the Factory—a place Soli knew well.

"What will we find when we get there?" Heddy asked.

"I don't know. But since Holst specifically requested my presence, he must want to discuss something about art history. The note was brief and didn't disclose any facts about what he's discovered or anything else."

"Wait," Heddy said as they arrived at a clearing overlooking a field. "That looks like an excavation site." She placed her hand in front of Soli, blocking her from continuing. "Do you see any German soldiers or suspicious-looking people around?"

"No, but there's bound to be Nazi-friendly folks here, just like everywhere else."

"I know. We just need to be prepared in case we must run. Be careful when you speak with these people."

"I will."

"Do you trust this professor?"

"Well, he used to be the head of the archaeology department at the university, and I learned a lot from him. He never seemed like the kind who'd abandon his country. Besides, he did say our *boys in the woods* had contacted him."

"*Milorg* wouldn't have approached him if he'd been Nazi; they wouldn't risk being caught." Heddy put the last piece of potato in her mouth. "But why did you take his classes when you studied art history?"

"The various fields of history are linked together. Somehow, they're all dependent upon archaeological digs and research."

"I understand." Heddy kept staring at two men shoveling the ground at the excavation site.

"You're worried." Soli said.

"Always, Soli. Wherever we go, there are dangers lurking around corners. After all, I recruited you to our clandestine organization."

Soli hooked her arm around Heddy's. "And you feel responsible for my safety."

Heddy nodded. "Something like that. But then again, we've been through a lot already, and you've taught the rest of us a thing or two about courage and perseverance."

"We're in this together and keep an eye on each other." Soli squeezed Heddy's arm. "Come. Let's speak with the professor first. Then we'll try to save the world later, all right?"

Heddy smiled back and adjusted her burgundy beret, tilting it slightly off-center. Her dark eyes and gorgeous smile with the bright-red lips would probably turn the heads of the workers at the site. But Heddy never paid attention to flirtatious men. She'd given her heart to Soli's brother Sverre, and even though he'd fled to Sweden, she only had eyes for him.

Oh, how Soli hoped for her brother to return soon to a free country. Lately, Hitler's war had not gone the Führer's way. There were rumors of capitulation now, but here they were, still living in a war zone with an unpredictable outcome. Sverre continued his undercover work from an apartment in Stockholm.

Off to the side of a swampy patch stood a forest-green

tent—the free-standing kind a team could easily pitch in any terrain. An older man with a neatly trimmed white mustache and a considerably bushy hairdo under his herringbone wool hat spun around as they approached. His calf-length, tweed coat covered the top of muddy boots. He had not changed much, except for an expression that appeared a bit more worn and tired.

"Soli. What a pleasure to see you again." He shook her hand with vigor then turned to her friend. His smile dropped. "I thought you'd come alone."

"Not to worry, Professor Holst. This is Heddy Vengen." Soli lowered her voice. "From what you wrote in your note, you wanted to keep this excavation confidential for now. Heddy assists me in my art business and is reliable in every way."

That last part was true to some point. Ever since Soli had joined the resistance to help save precious artwork from ending up in the Führer's collection, she and Heddy had been inseparable.

The professor regained his composure, and his skeptical frown faded. He grabbed Soli's arm. "Well then, my little art expert. Let me tell you and your friend why I've asked you to come."

"You know I'm no authority on archaeological finds."

"You'll change your mind once I've told you the rest of the story. I called you out here this morning because I believe we see eye to eye on this matter. I remember you well from your years at the university. You never gave up, determined as you were to complete an education despite restrictions. Do you recall when the German authorities shut down the university, blaming it on a fire in the grand hall? They claimed our students had tried to burn down the building. But we knew better. Instead, *Reichskommissar* Terboven held a thundering speech indicating the lack of Nazi sympathizers among our students and faculty."

"I'm glad you weren't arrested."

"Yes, but I was interrogated, mind you. Miraculously enough, I was allowed to continue my work, but sadly, many of my colleagues were imprisoned. My heart broke when I heard that two hundred and sixty students had been sent to camps in Germany."

His eyes became soft. "You, Soli, were such a young student and blessed to be left alone."

"My father called it stubborn."

"Haha...yes, I'd say you were. But the study of art history was your calling in life."

"It still is."

"I know how you feel, Soli. I have thoroughly enjoyed my studies abroad, working on digs in Egypt, Holland, Denmark, and even here in Norway as we discovered Viking ships."

"That must have been fascinating."

"Hmm...I was a young intern when we came across the Oseberg ship in 1904. What an adventure. The most splendid Viking grave ever unearthed. My health doesn't permit me to travel much now, and with the war going on, I mostly tinker with smaller projects."

"Do the Germans still leave you alone?"

"No, they show up whenever they have questions about old artifacts. They are seriously interested in finding hidden treasures." He steepled his hands and gave Soli a sideways glance. "Which brings me to why you're here. Not only are you highly gifted and knowledgeable, but I can trust you."

"Trust me? What's wrong?"

He wrung his hands and looked out on the marsh below. "What I'm about to tell you is confidential. In fact, this information is top secret. It won't topple kingdoms, but it has to do with keeping buried riches out of Hitler's plundering hands."

Heddy gave Soli a serious gaze. This was exactly the kind of thing they risked their lives for...time and again... and why Heddy had recruited Soli. Their part of the war effort was to diminish Nazi art theft.

"No Nazi or German officer must hear of this. Heaven knows they'd certainly want a piece of this dig."

Heddy leaned her shoulder bag against a stool and placed a hand on his arm. "You can trust us, Professor Holst. How may we help?"

"A group of our home-front boys came through the woodland and fields here a few days ago. As they crossed the marsh, they stumbled upon a skeleton. My nephew is one of those men, and since he didn't know who to turn to during these trying times, he told me to come have a look."

Holst gesticulated as he spoke, changing his voice from high to low. He was still the same as when he'd taught archaeology classes, only older. His theatrical way of combining history, facts, and legends had made every lesson both interesting and fun.

"A skeleton?" Heddy narrowed her brow. "Our country has been invaded for five years. Several hundred thousand German soldiers occupy our land. I don't mean to sound ignorant, but with the war still going on, I'd think we'd find skeletons in many places."

Holst put a finger in the air. "Ah, you're correct, but there's more."

Soli compressed her lips together. "You're not talking

about bones from our time, are you, Professor Holst? You wouldn't be investigating the grounds here if it didn't have significant historical interest."

The professor gave Soli a curt nod. "Exactly. This particular skeleton has a certain fascination for scholars like me. And when I show you what we've discovered, Soli, I'm sure you'll agree this is within your field of expertise, as well."

"I'm intrigued," Soli said with a smile.

Holst waved his hand. "Come inside, ladies."

He pushed the tent door open. A tarpaulin covered the ground in the middle and upon it a skeleton, fragments of textiles and black hair, metal weapons, other artifacts, and a round, tube-shaped, wooden container.

"You've moved the find?" Soli asked and stepped closer, squatting next to the canvas.

"Yes, we dug it up from the marsh on the field, but due to the soft and challenging terrain we had to set up our tents on more solid ground." He pulled his shoulders back and placed his hands on his hips. "Now, tell me what you see, Soli. What's your first impression?"

Soli walked around the oilcloth. "I see a man of medium height. His teeth are still intact. No fractures or bullets in his skull. A couple of his ribs look broken."

"Heddy, what does that mean to you?" Asking questions and making them think for themselves was the professor's way of teaching.

"He could have fallen or been in a fight," Heddy answered.

Holst smiled and nodded.

"And he has a sword." Soli leaned in closer. "It's a rapier, used in the seventeenth century by both civilians and military. When traveling alone, he could defend himself. It has a two-edged blade and is light enough to thrust with one hand. Notice the intricate, wide hilt. It protects the hand from cuts."

She glanced at the professor. He seemed pleased with her description so far.

"What about the smaller weapon there?" Heddy pointed to a metal knife with a long blade.

"A dagger." Soli frowned. "The combination of those two weapons is confusing. The workmanship of the rapier is exquisite, but the dagger looks homemade...like something a poor peasant would carry."

The professor lifted his eyebrow. "And...?"

"Well, either the man stole the rapier from someone, or..." She shook her head. "No, he was most likely a thief. A rich man would not have carried such a simple knife." She stood. "I'd say he traveled by foot as there's no sign of a horse among these things."

The professor clapped his hands. "My thoughts, too. You remember well."

Heddy smiled. "She remembers everything."

Holst walked around to the other side of the tarpaulin. "There are also remnants of a leather pouch and some coins. Those smaller bones come from a rabbit. Perhaps our man had it hanging from his belt and died before he had the chance to eat it."

Heddy frowned. "But how can something stay in the ground for that long and not decompose?"

"Not in normal ground, my dear. Soil would break down both body and clothing, but that marsh out there has been here for hundreds of years. A swamp like that is built gradually over time from layers and layers of dead organic material. With little or no oxygen, decomposition is extremely slow. Such peat bogs are amazing for preserving human remains. Archaeologists have uncovered people and animals much older than this fellow. I've worked on a couple of digs in Denmark. At one site, we found the body of a young woman from the early Iron Age. She had braided hair and a full-length cloak. Due to a rope and a furrow around her neck, we could even tell she'd been hanged. Close by, a few years later, we unearthed the remains of a man who was nine thousand years old. Such finds are most significant and teach us about life a long, long time ago."

Heddy raised her eyebrows. "Incredible. I can understand why you find your work so fascinating."

The professor's eyes glistened with enthusiasm. "Mud protects the same way. Our Viking ships were unusually well preserved in blue clay. But what would be interesting is glacier archaeology. Think about how much we could find in those ice-covered areas—bodies with tolls and weapons, animals—all frozen and prevented from decaying." Holst pointed to Soli. "I'm getting carried away here. Now, young lady. What time period are we talking about with our mystery man?"

"Mid-sixteen-hundreds."

A content smile formed on the professor's lips. "That's my girl!" He stepped closer. "You keep staring at that round tube next to our traveler. What are your thoughts on that?"

"That this item—or rather what's inside—is why you asked me to come." She kneeled on the canvas and carefully touched the wooden cylinder. "A container like this could hold an important map, valuable documents, or architectural drawings." She turned her head and met the

14

professor's gaze. "It could also contain a renaissance or baroque work of art."

"Yes, and that's why I need your help. The top of the tube is sealed with a thick layer of wax. There's a good possibility that whatever is inside is still intact. But on the other hand, a crack or slit somewhere would be detrimental. If the man traveled through rain or snow, he'd have a hard time keeping his belongings dry. Moisture breeds bacteria, and the items would surely rot or shrivel."

Heddy crouched to have a closer look at the pouch. "He could have journeyed far. What do the coins tell you?"

"You're learning fast. We found a few Dutch gulden."

Heddy stared at the wooden tube. "And that container would be an easy way to carry something, wouldn't it?"

"Yes, he probably tied it on his back or hung it across a shoulder to move swiftly through the terrain." Soli rose to her feet. "Although, I wouldn't advise to keep a map or a painting rolled up for longer periods. The paint can easily crack and peel over time. Less flexibility simply makes the dye brittle."

"The man probably never thought it would take three hundred years before the wooden tube was opened." Holst unfolded a small stool, sat down, and wiped his nose with a handkerchief. "But what if the inside is completely dry?"

Soli shrugged. "Then there's no telling how long an artwork can be preserved."

"What about paper?" Heddy asked.

"Paper contains more water and ages quicker than canvas," Soli answered. "At the time of our man here, paper was made of linen and cotton rags, and even if paper is less durable than a primed, damp-resistant canvas, it could probably stand the test of time if there's no humidity."

Heddy squinted. "So, the mystery man traveled alone, and he may have been in a hurry to reach his destination without any highway robbers or other thieves finding him. It must be something valuable. The craftmanship of that container is proof of that, isn't it?"

Soli peeked out through the opening of the tent. The workers were still at the site below. She reached her hand outside. Soft mist touched her skin. She closed the opening and returned to the others. "I can barely wait to see what's inside, but we shouldn't open the tube here. Damp air could cause whatever's inside to crumble before our eyes."

Holst nodded. "Exactly. I suggest we take it back to my laboratory."

"Yes, there or another safe place. It's imperative we keep this find quiet for now."

He pursed his lips. "Unfortunately, you're correct. At least until we know more about who our renaissance man is, and especially what's in the tube. The Reich collects every interesting and valuable treasure unto themselves. They'd show up here in an instant if they found out we were concealing a treasure map, a royal proclamation, or an important painting. My whole being is resisting such a confrontation. I'm not ready to hand this over...not yet."

Soli nodded. "We agree on that."

Holst stood, stretched his back, and exhaled a rapid breath. "I'll personally take the tube to my office today. How about you two come in this evening close to curfew, and we'll open it together?"

Heddy picked up her shoulder bag, ready to leave. "We'll be there."

"Thank you, Heddy." Holst grabbed both of Soli's hands. His eyes were filled with an almost fatherly emotion. "Our passions for archaeology and art history are entwined."

"Yes, they are, Professor Holst. I give you my word, Heddy and I will do our best to help."

CHAPTER TWO

OSLO, NORWAY

SOLI CHECKED HER wristwatch twice as they walked up Karl Johan's Street toward Professor Holst's office.

"It's past eight," she said. "Less than an hour before curfew."

Heddy nudged Soli's shoulder. "That should be enough time, unless you uncover wonderful things when you open the archaeologist's mysterious tube. Then we'll be up all night."

Soli lifted her eyebrows at her friend and smiled.

"Don't give me that mischievous grin, Soli. It wouldn't be the first time." Heddy sighed. "I don't mind. We live dangerously every day, and the adventures we've been on together have always been exciting."

"And frightening," Soli reminded her. "It hasn't been all fun and games."

"No, you're right. I'm just trying some of that Soli optimism. Your belief in victory has boosted my spirits many times."

"I could say the same about you." She stopped in front

of the entrance to an office block behind the university. "Here it is. His workplace is up on the second floor."

They climbed the rickety stairs and knocked on the door to the left. Within seconds, the professor answered. He stuck his head out to check if anyone else was around.

"Nosy neighbors. This office building houses all sorts. I have just one rule; trust only those who can be trusted."

He pulled them inside.

Heddy asked, "How's that rule working for you?"

"Basically, it means I trust hardly anyone."

He pointed to the table where the wooden cylinder lay on a white cotton sheet.

"There it is. I put some tools there, too." Holst stepped forward and put his hands on his hips. "Shall we?"

He used a small paring knife to cut through the edge of the wax sealing and a scalpel to push the substance aside. He pulled a pair of round-rimmed glasses from his breast pocket and placed them on the tip of his nose. "It's quite hard. I'd say they used a mixture of resin and beeswax on this. But look, there's some kind of mark here."

Soli leaned in. "It looks like an impression. Do you have a magnifying glass?"

"Yes, in the top drawer of the stand over there by the window."

"I'll get it." Heddy hurried to fetch the magnifying glass then handed it to Soli.

"Seals were used by many classes of society. They pressed a handheld seal onto hot wax, but this impression is fairly small. It may be from a signet ring." Soli held the magnifying glass over the stamp. "A ring like that was a symbol of power and status. It could be worn by high-ranking clergy. Royalty or aristocrats would use a wax ring with a stamp of a crown or their family coat-of-arms. Sometimes, they'd put their hand out and have people kiss their ring."

Heddy jerked her head back. "Are you saying someone higher up had the mystery man carry this tube all the way from the Netherlands to Norway?"

"I don't know...not yet."

The professor placed his hands on the table. "Could our man have stolen such a ring?"

Soli raised her head. "I've never read anywhere that a villain symbolically stole status by taking a ring."

"But what if the owner died?" Heddy asked.

"Then the authority would be transferred to his rightful heir. A ring could pass from father to son through several generations. If he had no heir, they most likely destroyed the ring to prevent fake seals."

"So, since a signet ring was mostly used as a mark of authority or identification, could a commoner own one?" Heddy asked.

"No, usually not. But if a merchant, politician, or anyone else of importance in society had to send a vital dispatch by coach or a messenger on horseback, they'd mark their correspondence using a simpler, handheld seal with their monogram."

Soli bowed her head again, holding the magnifying glass above the imprint. "It looks like a W. Just one letter."

Heddy put her palms up. "And...?"

"It's not a royal or noble seal. But let's open the tube all the way. I can't wait to see what's inside."

"How about this idea?" the professor asked enthusiastically. "Would a band of thieves—even gentleman thieves —keep such a wax seal or an emblem of their own? I know it's irregular, but anything is possible. I'd like to research this some more. One of my former students became a historian, perhaps he—"

Soli shook her head. "No, we can't involve more people. It would be interesting to find out more, even have an exact date for when he traveled through our woods, but not now."

The professor nudged Heddy and winked. "She's strict, isn't she?" He adjusted the glasses on his nose again and carefully removed the beeswax lid, keeping the impression of the seal intact. "Well, Miss Soli, tell us what you see."

She pulled out some straw around the edges inside. "After the grain and chaff were removed, dry stalks like this would be used to contain any moisture and to prevent whatever's inside from being damaged. A frail piece of paper or a painting could chafe if it continually jolted against the inner edges."

Soli's heart thundered against her chest as she pulled out a roll wrapped in a thin linen shroud. The professor rapidly moved the container, knife, and pieces of wax to the side of the table, and Heddy smoothed the cotton material.

With great care Soli folded the linen aside and unrolled the canvas onto the sheet.

The room went completely quiet. An exquisite rendition of a musketeer lay on the table before them. The man looked as if he was in his early thirties. He had chin-length, wavy hair under a wide-brimmed hat with feathers and ribbons and seemed to look directly at them with determined, dark eyes.

"I'll say...he is incredibly good looking," Heddy blurted eagerly. "Gauntlets on his hands...and that stylish mustache. He reminds me of pictures I've seen of—" She snapped her fingers. "I can't remember what they're called...you know, the soldiers who protected the king of France a long time ago."

"Musketeers," Soli said, goosebumps springing up over her arms. "Yes, I believe he is one."

The professor looked closer. "But he's wearing a loose, soft shirt and wide breeches tucked into bucket-topped boots. Why is he not portrayed with the tabard with an embroidered white cross? His pose is quite relaxed, standing there with his woolen cloak flung across his right shoulder as if he can conquer the world."

"He has plenty of weapons, though," Heddy said and pointed to a leather belt around the man's waist holding both pistol and dagger. "And he carries a rifle and a sword."

"That rifle is the musket of that time, Heddy. Armed soldiers with muskets called themselves musketeers." Holst looked at Soli. "But you think he was in the personal household guard of the French king, don't you?"

Soli nodded.

"How can you tell?" Heddy asked.

The thrill of their discovery made Soli forget the war, forget how, every single day, she and Heddy avoided the horrible Gestapo and ruthless enemy soldiers. Here and now, she could not help but smile and enjoy the moment. "That's the beauty of art, isn't it? Not only can we admire craftmanship and brushstrokes from the past, but we learn about life before our time. I believe this man was in the service of King Louis XIII."

Heddy widened her eyes. "How can you be so precise?"

"I can tell by his clothes and also this." She pointed to

a round emblem dangling from the hilt of the man's sword.

"Ah, that is a good indication," the professor said. "A silver coin." He squinted and leaned closer. "LVDOVIC-S.XIII. And there's the fleur-de-lys engraved in the middle. Oh, this is exciting. Ludvig, or Louis in French, became king as a nine-year-old and had the notion to build a hunting lodge south of Paris overlooking the old town of Versailles." Holst burst out laughing. "The king was dissatisfied and had his builder replace it with what we now know as the Palace of Versailles. King Louis was powerful, rich, and remarkable in many ways."

"I believe the artist added the coin to show who this musketeer was loyal to, but also as an indication that the man was well-to-do, possibly a diplomat or an emissary of the crown on the side." Soli straightened. "Which brings us to who painted the portrait."

The professor and Heddy stared at her.

"Rembrandt. See the small signature there in the bottom right corner?"

"Another Rembrandt. This is amazing," Heddy said.

"What do you mean another one?" the professor asked, a suspicious but curious look in his eyes.

Soli paused. She trusted Professor Holst, but in case he was ever interrogated about his finds, the less information he had about her previous clandestine operations, the better. "Oh, we've seen another painting by Rembrandt, but let's concentrate on this one now," she said, hoping he'd buy her brief explanation.

The professor seemed to understand and let the matter be. "Moving on then…from what I remember, Rembrandt signed his name in several ways during his career."

Soli nodded. "That's right. This signature is spelled with a D, something the artist did after 1633."

"How do we know this is an original, not a fake, or even the work of one of his pupils?"

"Look for the *chiaroscuro*—the play with light and dark against each other. Study the brushstrokes. Rembrandt often used an impasto technique and applied a good amount of paint, so we can see the paint physically stand out from the canvas. His brushstrokes become more visible as they catch light from different angles. He also added fast-drying pigments to his mixtures. See the detailed strands of hair escaping the hat there? Rembrandt used a sharpened brush to scratch the wet paint to create such an illusion. He experimented with colors and glazes to master the difference in transparency and opacity in his paintings. But he was an artist with a need for variation and changed his techniques depending on the effect he desired." She paused and smiled. "Oh, I could go on and on. He was truly the most significant painter in Dutch history, one of the greatest in all of Europe."

Heddy crossed her arms. "This may be a silly question —I know we've discussed old portraits before—but didn't these old masters paint mostly religious or mythological paintings at this time? They did royal portraits, also, but why a musketeer?"

"No, it's not silly at all," Soli said. "That's a great question, and there's a simple explanation why this man would have his portrait done. During the Renaissance period, the Catholic leaders ordered artwork for their enormous cathedrals with side chapels that required many altarpieces. After the reformation, the simpler protestant churches didn't have the same amount of decorations. Artists lost their steady income from the church. What were they to do? Fortunately, Amsterdam was filled with rich traders and merchants who wanted portraits of themselves and their families. Master artists like Rembrandt received new and interesting orders for such depictions."

"Ah, that makes sense."

Soli turned the canvas over. "We still don't know who this handsome man is."

Heddy pointed to a few letters in the top left corner. "Here's something. AR & CB." She glanced at Soli. "Is it too much of a coincidence?"

Narrowing his brow, Holst leaned forward on the table. "What kind of coincidence? Do you know who the model is?"

Soli turned the painting back to the front. "I'm sorry, Professor, but Heddy and I believe strongly that we shouldn't say anything more right now."

"But—"

Heddy put her hand on his arm. "For your own safety."

Holst gave a casual shrug. "Well, I know all about keeping secrets, don't I?"

Soli smiled. "Yes, you do. This one is ours, and we'll tell you everything one day, I promise. But for now, please let me do some research. I want to ask you to trust me enough to take this painting and hide it until later tonight to make sure the Germans don't get a hold of it."

"Where will you take it then?"

"We can't tell you that, either. Not now. There are certain German officers who actively seek valuable art for Hitler's collection. Let's not let them have this one. Most of all, as we said, for your own protection you're better off not knowing."

"I understand." He sat down on a chair and wiped his brow with a handkerchief. "There are too many soldiers out on Karl Johan's Street this time in the evening. How about you pick it up here early tomorrow morning before the town wakes up? I'll find a proper crate for the painting."

Soli lightly touched the professor's shoulder. "That would be excellent. Now that the coats of paints have been exposed to fresh oxygen again, it would be best not to roll it up as tightly as it was. Do you have a container large enough to lay it flat?"

"I have several such crates already. I'll be sure to wrap it properly for safe travel wherever you're taking it. Do you have a car?"

"That won't be a problem," Heddy said.

"Good. Then when you return tomorrow morning, be quick about it, and drive off immediately."

"Perfect. We'll do that."

Soli glanced at the clock on the wall. Almost nine. "It's time to go. We don't want to break curfew." She turned to the professor. "We only noticed two people at the dig with you. Is that correct?"

"Yes, only the two. I tried to limit the number of assistants."

"And other than that? Who knows about this find?" Heddy asked.

"Only the Milorg boys who found the skeleton. They are reliable chaps."

Heddy nodded. "If they weren't, we'd have little resistance left in this country." She shook Holst's hand. "We'll be back in a few hours. Stay safe."

Soli hugged the professor. "Thank you for remembering me. I'll never forget this day."

* * *

Out on the street, Soli hooked her arm around Heddy's, and they turned left on the corner of Karl Johan's Street.

She leaned in and whispered as they walked. "AR has to be Annarosa Ruber, the foremother of the Jewish family who used to live on Oscar Street behind the royal palace."

"I agree. It's from the same time period as some of their other portraits and the same artist as the last one we found. Oh, what I'd give to end this war and bring the Ruber family back from deportation. They should live in their beautiful house and be free with their family and their treasured artwork." She squeezed Soli's arm. "But you still have the Ruber family's old ledger in your basement. Can you do some research and see if you find a transaction for this painting in there?"

"I'll examine it meticulously. Hopefully, I'll discover something about that fine-looking musketeer." Soli walked a bit slower. "Did we do the right thing, Heddy? It was hard to tear myself away and leave the painting there."

They stepped to the side to pass a group of German soldiers. Some were out on patrol; others seemed to be out on an evening walk in downtown Oslo. Soli always held her breath when she had close encounters with the enemy and looked straight ahead so as not to draw any attention to herself.

Safely rounding a corner farther down, Soli leaned closer. "The professor was right. Carrying a large wooden crate around town would be suspicious. And I couldn't tell him about the art club, our boys, and what we do."

Heddy agreed. "He has the same problem as we do; three hundred and eighty thousand German occupants and not knowing who to trust among our own people. Who sides with the enemy? Who is genuinely stalwart and strong against the Wehrmacht? Maybe even more confusing is that some men and women have a neutral state of mind. They follow the wind and eventually tip one way or another. Your decision was clear. It was the right thing to say, Soli."

"Good. I didn't want to hurt his feeling, but he understands. In his line of work, he deals with similar challenges. We work with the underground in Oslo and make sure art treasures don't end up in the wrong hands, so to speak. He tries to keep the Gestapo away from his work. He probably knows much more about archaeological treasures hidden from the Germans than he lets on. In case things go wrong with our musketeer painting, we don't want Holst to be interrogated by the Germans, caught up in Minister President Quisling's wicked yarn, or harassed by Nazi art dealers."

"And lest—heaven forbid—the professor should prove to be an unfaithful servant and run off with the painting, he shouldn't know where we've hidden other artwork."

Soli shuddered. "The thought has crossed my mind, but I really don't think he'd switch sides."

"I believe you're right." Heddy bit her lip and gave Soli a probing look. "I have a question."

"Only one?"

Heddy covered her face with her hands. "I know...but I always try to understand how the pieces fit together. Let's say the man in the marsh was not a thief. What if the skeleton is the musketeer...that he is the man in the painting? Have you thought about that?"

"I have. But then I remembered the strands of raven-black hair next to the skeleton, the remnants of his clothes, and the cheap knife. The musketeer in the painting had brown hair and wore clothing of finer materials." She paused. "But there's more that puzzles me. Why did the man carry the painting across a swampland in Norway, and where was he going? After all, the portrait originates from Amsterdam. I'd also like to discover when the Ruber family arrived in Norway. It would be interesting to find out and connect the dots."

"As I'm sure you will. But first, we need to hide the painting for a while. I promise you'll have plenty of time to study it later."

Soli didn't look forward to sending the portrait off already. But Heddy was right. They had to send it out of Oslo to a safer place.

They passed the *Storting* with the enormous banner on the front. *Deustchland siegt an allen Fronten.* Soli certainly hoped Germany would not be victorious on all fronts. A slight breeze pushed them along and tugged at the red flags hanging from stores and office buildings along the street. The black swastika on a white circle gave her an eerie feeling every time, even after five years. Could the rumors about a possible end to the wretched war be true? She prayed every day it was close at hand.

Three German soldiers on the other side of the street whistled at Soli and Heddy as they stopped to say goodbye. Soli turned her back to them and grimaced.

"Don't let them bother you," Heddy said. "They're just young men wanting attention."

"I know. It's still uncomfortable." Soli put her arms around Heddy. "I need to hurry home and study the ledger. Meet you outside Professor Holst's office tomorrow morning at five?"

"Sure. I'll have the boys bring the car."

CHAPTER THREE

SOLI ENTERED BY her back door. She kicked off her shoes and tossed her beret and coat onto the couch. Since she'd inherited the art shop the year before, her workroom—where she built custom frames and mounted art pieces—had also become her home.

Even though the room had a sink, a cupboard, and a sofa she slept on, it was still a studio. Frames leaned against the walls, some empty, others displaying etchings and paintings. In the middle was a workbench the size of a dining table with current projects and orders. Thin glass, matt board, narrow black strips of wood molding, a box containing glue and tacks, corner clamps, and a small hammer—everything she needed to make quality mounts for her customers.

She didn't mind living there. It was far better than sleeping in the attic at her aunt and uncle's apartment. This was her home now, and she could come and go as she pleased. Well, not exactly. Restrictions, curfew, and the never-ending encounters with German soldiers on the streets were not what she called freedom. The constant feeling of being on the edge of panic was probably the worst. The dread that members of the Gestapo would show up and drag her away for being part of the resistance, for fighting Hitler and his regime. Anxiety that someone would start investigating, interrogate her, and discover where she'd hidden precious artwork from Nazi collectors.

She grabbed a piece of bread from the cupboard and walked out into the small hallway leading to the shop. On the left was an office, and on the right was a door that led to the basement. She unlocked the door and climbed down the creaking staircase to a long storage room. Since she often changed the pictures in the showroom and the window display toward the street, the cellar housed art for different seasons, art done in various techniques, and those conveying various moods. Not that she'd organized the space. A visitor would surely find her underground store a horrible mess, but Soli usually located what she was looking for.

She pushed aside a bookcase on the left wall to reveal a hidden door. The key needed a certain twist to turn. She pulled the handle and opened. Even weeks after she'd taken over the shop, the secret chamber had given her mixed feeling—mostly dread and horror—but also a despondent admittance to how greed can change a person to commit horrible acts. If those walls could speak, people would be appalled.

Since then, her downstairs office had housed a runaway Jew, had preserved important artwork and documents, and now, Soli hid the Ruber family's ledger here, safely wrapped in a clean linen cloth and placed in a locked chest. For three-hundred-and-fifty years, the Jewish family had kept an account of their acquisitions in the old book. Her goal was to safeguard the ledger and keep it out of the hands of anyone who'd want to steal the Ruber art collection, either for the Reich or their own personal gain.

Soli had browsed the old book many times before and had been able to find hidden paintings purchased by the merchant Isaac Ruber of the seventeenth century, his daughter Fabiola, and his granddaughter Annarosa. Soli had already found three of these paintings and placed them somewhere safe with good help from Heddy's group. She cringed to think how the Jewish family was gone now, deported on a ship out of the country like cattle, and their belongings confiscated. Soli's sweetheart, Nikolai Lange, had said there was not much chance of their return. Everyone in the Ruber family had been taken away, all except one: Jacob Ruber, whom they'd helped flee across the border to Sweden.

Her Nikolai was a police investigator with deep-blue eyes, a dimpled chin, and a boyish smile. Thinking about her handsome detective made her heart beam. He'd walked into the store and her life on a day filled with nothing but trouble. The cleaning lady had been found dead in the side alley, and Soli, although upset about the poor woman's misfortune, was more frustrated than helpful in Nikolai's investigation.

Her Nikolai. Luckily, he'd seen past that horrible first meeting and Soli's behavior. She'd pushed the embarrassment away and had given in. It wasn't difficult. They'd found a connection, a long-awaited embrace, a soft kiss, and kind words. Soli had fallen, and now...now she could proclaim to the world: She loved Nikolai Lange.

She wiped her hands on a clean towel and unlocked the chest by the wall. On top was a small pile of her own amateurish drawings and watercolors from school. She was no artist. It was the history she found interesting and the lives of the master painters. Who wouldn't revel in spending time interpreting and understanding the development of art, determining how to decide which artist could be attributed, and learning about technique and medium? It had to do with culture, symbols, and icons. It included styles and artistic movements. Passion would be the right word to describe how she felt about the world of art history—an interest Soli had enjoyed since she was a little girl, what she'd spent years studying, and what now caused her great danger as she was deep into resistance work.

She moved her simple artwork aside, put on a pair of white cotton gloves she kept there, and carefully picked up the ledger. Seated on a stool with wheels, Soli placed the book on the desk and admired the leather binding carved with an elaborate border of leaves and geometric shapes. Most of the gold tooling was intact, and the gilded edges were still beautiful. She opened the brass locket like she'd done several times before. How grateful she was that Nikolai had placed the book in her care to peruse and decipher the clues written among the rows of purchases and sales. Studying such a precious volume filled her with awe.

The opening page always made her pause and draw a deep breath.

*Inventario degli acquisti e delle vendite del commerciante
Isaac Ruber
La Valletta, Malta, 4 dicembre 1573.*

1573! The Italian merchant Isaac Ruber of Valetta, Malta was the first to record the family's trades and purchases of china, porcelain, jewelry, and—most importantly to Soli—artwork by renowned master painters. Caravaggio. Rubens. Rembrandt. Soli sighed. The ledger was a treasure chest of what life had been like for the wealthy, Jewish-Italian family. Soli straightened her back. No time to dream and dawdle. The wonderful Rembrandt portrait of the handsome musketeer...that's what she should concentrate on. The back of the canvas had the initials AR and CB. The first had to be Annarosa Ruber, the merchant's granddaughter. But who was CB?

She poured over the pages Annarosa had kept, starting with the year 1639. Thank goodness, Soli had learned some Italian during her art studies. Being able to read and learn about this ancient family was a privilege.

Suddenly, she stopped at a fresh leaf.

Beni acquisiti tramite il mio matrimonio con Claude Beaulieu nell'anno 1640.

Claude Beaulieu? This name was new to her. *Acquisition through my marriage to Claude Beaulieu in the year 1640.* Claude Beaulieu had to be CB from the painting.

Soli continued down the side. Her heart skipped a beat as she read the next line.

Claude Beaulieu al servizio di Sua Maestà il Re Luigi XIII di Francia. Ritratto del suo amico Rembrandt, 1637.

Then written in the margin with bold letters: *Rubato, 1641.*

Soli read the words again. *Stolen, 1641.*

The musketeer portrait was taken from Annarosa and her husband Claude in the seventeenth century. A masterpiece painted by Claude's friend Rembrandt. It felt as if Soli's insides were vibrating. *The musketeer was Rembrandt's friend.*

Annarosa had included nothing regarding her suspicions or thoughts on who the bandit was. Only that it was stolen. Soli's theory could be correct. Was the skeleton the professor had dug up from the marsh really a Dutch thief?

She closed the ledger and leaned back. Enough for now. The musketeer had a name, and he'd married into the prosperous Ruber family in Amsterdam. But, somehow, this portrait had found its way to a northern country. Her arms and legs tingled with curiosity. What had happened?

Good thing they had not told the professor about the other paintings they'd already found. For his own safety, he'd be better off kept in the dark about the musketeer portrait, as well.

THURSDAY, 26 APRIL 1945

CHAPTER FOUR

IN THE EARLY morning hours, Soli waited outside Professor Holst's office. Fortunately, the streets were still empty. Only a few men walked by, carrying fishing poles or lunch boxes. Norwegians and Germans worked together at the Aker Shipyard, producing machine equipment for boats. Only a few months earlier, the factory had been hit by the largest sabotage maneuver to date. Knowing how important it was for the Germans to keep both military and civilian ships in order, a resistance group had destroyed four vessels and damaged the pier. Some of Soli's friends had been involved, and the long night she'd spent wondering if they'd gotten away, constantly praying for their safe return, was etched into her memory.

She expected Birger and Arvid to drive up in their truck. Heddy's boys were ever willing to help out. But when a black car stopped next to the entrance, Soli backed up, ready to walk away. The Gestapo had cars like that.

She didn't want any trouble or questions about what she was doing out on the street so early.

"Soli!"

Nikolai jumped out from the driver's seat.

She turned and ran toward him, throwing her arms around his neck, hugging him fiercely.

"You scared me? What car is this?"

"It's one we have at the police station. I borrowed it."

"You borrowed it?"

He kissed her gently. "Don't worry. I'll return the vehicle within half an hour."

"But why are you here?"

"Not happy to see me?" He passed her a sideways glance and winked.

"Silly. I'm forever glad to see you."

"That's the right answer."

"But why aren't the boys here, Nikolai?" She relaxed her shoulders. "Heddy arranged this, didn't she? That woman is always on top of things. Does she ever sleep?"

"Probably less than a lot of people. She also takes way too many chances, walking around late at night by herself."

"I know. So, what did she tell you?"

"She gave me a brief description of your excursion yesterday. Something about a clandestine archaeological dig, a skeleton, and a mysterious wooden tube that contained a painting."

"Yes, it's a perfect and beautiful rendition of a seventeenth century musketeer. I hate to part with it so quicky, but we need to get it out of Oslo."

"That's where I come in. I'll take the painting to Birger and Arvid. They're waiting on the outskirts of town. The boys will speed up to Kongsberg right away and get the artwork to our friend, Thor Hammer."

"Good. Thor will hide it in the vault in the silver mines with the other paintings we've rescued. I hope all goes well."

"Don't worry. We'll take the portrait to safety before anyone notices."

Soli sighed. "Good. These operations squeeze my heart to pieces every time. I don't think I'll ever get used to it."

"Well, we constantly need to be on alert." He raked the area with his gaze. "Where's Heddy?"

"I don't know. She was supposed to be here ten minutes ago."

"Maybe she's already upstairs. I say we run up and get the artwork now. Waiting too long might cause a problem. There are several groups of soldiers only a few streets from here."

"One moment." Soli ran and checked around the corner. No Heddy.

Nikolai waved her back. "Come on," he called low.

They walked up the stairs and knocked on the door. They waited a few seconds and tried again. Nikolai pulled the handle and pushed the door open.

The office was vacant. The professor's desk was covered with papers as it had been the night before. Shelves of books, photographs of digs and exhibitions, even the open boxes with various artifacts seemed untouched. Everything looked the same, but where was the portrait? They checked every corner, closet, and the storage room behind his desk. Nothing. No painting. No newly built crate to transport the artwork. The only thing they found was the hollow, wooden tube, a treasure by itself since it dated so far back in time.

"Where are the professor and Heddy?" Soli asked.

Frowning, Nikolai ran his fingers through his dark hair. "I don't like the looks of this. Heddy wouldn't leave without telling us."

"Maybe she saw someone coming and hid with the professor and the painting." Soli pressed a hand to her chest. "Oh, how could this happen? We should have taken the portrait to my shop yesterday. My secret room downstairs would be a safe—"

Nikolai took hold of her hands and kissed them. "No, Soli. Don't look back. Last night would not have been the right moment to carry a large box or that old wooden tube through town. There were soldiers everywhere, and the risk of being stopped and questioned was too great. You could be sitting in a cell right now, my darling."

"But this is the second time, Nikolai."

"What do you mean?"

"I read in the ledger last night that this portrait was stolen. I believe it happened in Amsterdam around the year 1640." She rubbed her forehead.

"This is not your fault, Soli."

"It certainly feels that way."

He let go of her hands, walked over to the window, and pulled the blackout curtain slightly aside to look out. "We must hurry. I'll let Birger and Arvid know we've had a change of plans. You should return to the shop and hope Heddy shows up soon."

She slipped her arms around his waist and lay her head against his chest. "I need to hold you—just for a moment."

He enfolded Soli in a warm embrace then released her. "Is it possible the professor has run off with the portrait?"

"No, I've a hard time believing he'd do such a thing.

He asked for my help. We had a mutual trust and understanding and were both interested in safekeeping the painting."

"You're saying he's not the kind of archaeologist who keeps the treasures he unearths unto himself?"

"Not at all. His intentions have always seemed noble and honest."

"There's so much happening. You'd think our invaders would slow down their aggressive warfare now that the pressure is on Hitler. But we're still living with the looming danger of war hanging over our heads. Just yesterday, fifty-three civilians were killed in a bomb raid only a few miles from here. I drove down after it had happened. The bomb destroyed more than thirty houses. People were looking for their loved ones in the ruins. It was a horrible sight."

Soli was at a loss for words. Would it never end?

Nikolai led her down the stairs. Before they exited, he gave her a quick but tender kiss. "Be careful, my darling. There are still too many enemy soldiers in this country who raise their right arm in a *Sieg Heil* to the Führer. We are far from free...not yet."

"Free. A beautiful word...and a state of being I long to experience again."

He walked outside, checked up and down the street, and climbed into the car. Soli stood in the doorway as he drove off. The thrill of picking up the musketeer portrait and sending it off to be hidden in the silver mines had been dampened. Had Heddy and the professor taken it to a hiding place or—? She gasped and covered her mouth with her hand. What if this was another move by Lieutenant Colonel Heinz Walter? What a thorn in her side that man was. Not only was he a high-ranking officer of

the occupying forces, but Walter was also a most
dangerous man with his own agenda. As if they didn't
have enough problems already. Could the lieutenant
colonel be responsible for the disappearance of Heddy and
the professor? Soli bit her lip. Who had the Rembrandt
now?

CHAPTER FIVE

AFTER SHE CLOSED the shop, Soli walked through town to see Professor Holst's wife. A white picket fence surrounded the small garden, and even though the ground was still cold and barren, a promise of an approaching spring was evident in the well-kept beds. She entered the fence gate and knocked on the door.

A short woman with soft gray curls encircling her gentle face answered. "May I help you?"

"Mrs. Holst, my name is Soli Hansen. The professor was my teacher some years ago, and I'm currently working with him on a project. But as I went to meet him at his office today, he wasn't in. Is he here?"

"No, I'm afraid not," the woman said. She tipped her head. "I remember you from a small gathering we had for the students a few years ago."

"That's right. You'd baked the most delicious sponge cake with real wheat flour, not the kind we eat nowadays with mostly ground, boiled potatoes."

"Good ingredients make all the difference." She

opened the door wide. "Please come in. It seems like I'm eating dinner alone today. I don't understand why my husband is late."

Mrs. Holst showed Soli into a bright kitchen with yellow curtains. They seemed to match the old lady's personality. She set another plate on the table—blue and white china on a floral tablecloth.

"Please sit, Soli. It's a simple meal, but I suppose we're all used to that."

"Cabbage rolls. One of my favorite dishes."

"Well, there's no meat in these, but I made do, filling them with potatoes and whatever else I had."

"Thank you. This is food fit for a queen compared to what I've eaten lately."

Mrs. Holst removed her apron and sat down opposite Soli at the small, square kitchen table. She served them both, lifted her fork to take a bite but then stopped, holding the food in mid-air. "I'm quite worried about him. He was gone all day yesterday and then all night. Mind you, that's happened before when he's been caught up on a project. Sometimes, he can't tear himself away. To quote my husband, he finds his work 'a thrilling adventure'."

"I know the feeling."

Although pleasant, Soli didn't like where this conversation was headed. Professor Holst had not been home for two days.

"Has he been gone this long before?"

"No, and he knows that even if he's only half an hour late, I'll be concerned. My husband is an archaeologist and explorer, but he's always watchful and attentive to my needs." Mrs. Holst took a bite. "If you think you know where he could be, please tell me."

Soli could not make up stories about where the

professor was, although her imagination was running wild. The worst scenario was that Holst had been captured by Nazi art hunters, hurt, interrogated, or even worse...killed.

"I'm sorry...I don't, but he was in his office yesterday evening. All was well then."

Mrs. Holst sniffled a bit. She pushed her plate aside and placed her folded hands on the table. "So, that's something. But if you—"

"I'll try to find him, and of course, I'll let you know if I do." She reached out and laid her hands on the old woman's folded ones. "Try not to lose sleep over this."

"Oh, my dear. I'm an expert worrier."

They finished their supper and spoke of ration cards and long lines at the grocery store. Mrs. Holst proudly showed photographs of their five grandchildren and told Soli how she'd met her husband.

After a cup of tea, Soli picked up her shoulder bag. "I must go. Thank you so much for a lovely meal and the pleasant conversation."

"Please come again, dear. My days are rather lonely. Our daughters live out of town, and I don't see my grand-children that often."

"I will." Soli made a mental note of her answer and hoped it wouldn't be long before she could honor that promise.

"Be careful as you leave," Mrs. Holst said. "At the beginning of the war, a group of German soldiers moved into an apartment we have in the basement. We couldn't refuse. You know what it's like. In a skirmish with some of our home fighters, grenades and explosives were placed in the garden. After that, the invaders moved out. My husband and I haven't used that part of the plot since. I only tend the flower beds right next to the door here. Hopefully, one day, someone who knows what they're doing will come and remove the deadly weapons from our property."

"I'm so sorry, but on the other hand, you're probably elated the soldiers don't live in your house anymore."

"True. You always look for the good, don't you?"

"I try, but it's not always easy. In a way, I'm braver now but also more afraid than ever before. Does that make sense?"

"Yes, it does. Now, stay on the pathway to the gate, and you'll be safe."

"May I hug you?"

Mrs. Holst threw her arms around Soli. "Of course, dear girl. I hope the next time we see each other it is with good news that my husband is unharmed and sound."

* * *

Safely home, Soli plonked down on the couch. She had no idea where the Rembrandt musketeer painting was. But more troublesome than that, where were Professor Holst and Heddy?

Soli had expected a note from her friend, some sign that she'd been by. Maybe Heddy would show up later, but after an hour's waiting there was still nothing.

Soli pulled her feet up on the couch and hugged her legs. Oh, that this day were over and done. What was she to do? Where could she start looking for Holst and Heddy? Were the two even connected? That would be strange, but at this point, anything was possible.

Having the painting disappear so quickly left her with a knot in her stomach. That lovely Rembrandt rendition, flawless and precious. Oh, that she had it in her secret chamber in the basement right now. She'd go downstairs and study it for hours, putting herself in the master painter's time, imagining what it was like in Rembrandt's studio with the handsome, French musketeer modelling for his portrait.

Startled by a sound, Soli put her feet on the floor and sat up straight. Someone was at the back door. Two knocks twice. Only her friends at the secret art club or Nikolai rapped like that. She quickly went to answer.

"Oh, Nikolai." She grabbed his arm and pulled him inside. "I'm so glad you're here. I spent the evening with Professor Holst's wife, and she hadn't heard from her husband since yesterday morning. The painting is gone. And Heddy...where is she?"

"Come sit." He seated himself on the sofa and patted the next cushion. "Birger and Arvid haven't heard anything either."

She settled next to him. "You look serious, Nikolai. What do you know?"

"Lieutenant Colonel Heinz Walter has returned."

"No. Not this, as well. Why can't that horrible man just stay in Germany?"

"He travels to find art pieces. Every time he thinks he has discovered something of value here, he shows up, bringing death and fear with him."

"I hoped I never had to face him again."

"Well, I think you should prepare yourself. Walter will most likely speak with the different gallery owners and art connoisseurs like yourself. He usually does."

Soli sighed. "I can't close the shop and run off every time he comes."

"Tempting as that sounds, it would look suspicious."

Nikolai paused for a moment, resting his deep-blue eyes on her. "There's more," he said. "One of my men spotted the lieutenant colonel on the street outside Professor Holst's office early this morning."

Soli frowned. "How early?"

"Before we arrived."

Soli jumped up and started pacing the room. "But that could mean...no...oh, Nikolai, did he see anything else?"

Nikolai shook his head. "Only that a car drove up and stopped by the entrance. Walter and a couple of his men walked into the building. My officer was on his way to work and didn't think more about it at the time. My man had no idea what Walter was after. He only mentioned it in a briefing we had later this afternoon."

"And you had to keep calm about the incident?"

"Yes, and it's a struggle every day. Since the German occupants seized our police headquarters, they've arrested countless Norwegians for disobedience to the new regime. Even British citizens suspected of being secret agents have been incarcerated in the prison behind the office building. We can house about one hundred and fifty people there, but I've seen as many as five hundred or more crammed into the cells." He grunted. "I need to lead my men by obeying the German regulations. The police force at 19 Moller Street is a combination of Nazi supporters and true Norwegians—not that they speak about it—but after working with them for years, I've learned to read which side they're on."

Soli touched his cheek. "You live a dangerous life, Nikolai Lange. You attend special events arranged by the Gestapo and leaders of the Nazi party, and in between, you're collaborating with the resistance. How do you do it? You must be a great actor."

He flashed that special smile that always made her knees go weak. "I don't think Hollywood is ready for me, but I admit it takes a lot of concentration on my part, keeping the two roles separate and distinct. Fortunately, I've managed so far."

"But it's not safe."

He shrugged. "Says you. The work you, Heddy, and the boys do is no walk in the park, either." His face turned serious. "What are we going to do about Walter?"

"Well, we know from experience that the lieutenant colonel seeks art for his own benefit, not necessarily for Hitler's collection."

"And with his enemies closing in around him, I'd say he's more determined than ever to use his influence to find a few last pieces to increase his own wealth. His rank and uniform spread fear in people, and he has an entourage of men to support him and soldiers who will obey his every order. I'm sure he'll use his power for all it's worth."

"Not encouraging, but true. You forgot about his womanizing attitude," Soli said, shuddering at the mere thought.

Nikolai put his arm around Soli's shoulder. "Yes, that, too. Something you've witnessed."

"Unfortunately." She wrung her hands in her lap. "But I'm fine. Really, I am."

"Are you sure?"

She nodded. "I'm willing to continue our fight against him and all he stands for."

Nikolai rose to his feet. "I'm starving. How about you?"

She shook her head. "No, thank you. Mrs. Holst shared her dinner with me. Cabbage rolls."

"Mmm. I haven't had those in a while."

"Yes, they were so good." Soli flipped her hand. "But you go ahead. There's not much, but you can have whatever you find."

Nikolai collected a hard-boiled egg, a couple of pieces of bread, and some cheese from the cupboard. He put the food on a plate and sat down on the sofa next to Soli.

"The way I see it, there are two options. Either Heddy and the professor noticed Walter's arrival and have fled with the Rembrandt, or—"

Soli interrupted him. "Or the Germans have stolen the painting and have taken our friends somewhere." She covered her mouth. "What if—?"

Nikolai put his hand on her arm. "No, we'll find them. I'll put one of my best men on the case. He's proven trustworthy many times. We must believe they're alive. And no matter how precious this portrait is to you, the artwork comes secondary when people's lives are at stake."

"Undeniably so."

"If we're lucky, Heddy and the professor will show up with the painting. But if they don't, we'll do our best to find them...and the Rembrandt, as well. Walter can't be allowed to profit from looting art pieces that belong to the Ruber family's collection."

Nikolai finished eating and put the plate on the worktable. He leaned back, stretched his long legs under the coffee table, and pulled Soli into the corner of his arm. His sobering words had calmed her many times and had helped her stand firmly on the ground when her impulsive nature had her flying in every direction. At this moment, words were unnecessary. She closed her eyes, allowing Nikolai's presence to protect and emotionally nurture her being. They shared a bond, an unspoken pledge they belonged together.

Nikolai planted a soft kiss on her lips then slowly pulled his arm away. "I should leave."

He stood and put on his hat and trench coat. "Now, if you have any problems—anything at all—don't hesitate to call on me. I'll come as fast as I can."

"I know you will. But first, we need to find out what happened this morning."

He stroked her cheek. "Heddy has nine lives. She'll be fine."

"I hope you're right."

Soli locked the door behind him as he left. The room became awfully empty and quiet. Sleep would be welcomed now. This day had brought on enough problems and worries, and she just wanted it over and done with. Yet, uncomfortable thoughts about the German officer churned in her mind. Nikolai had told her to be prepared, but how could she prepare herself for a visit from Walter? The only thing she and the lieutenant colonel had in common was a love of fine art. Other than that, they were two opposites in a dangerous war.

~ CAPITOLO II ~

ANNAROSA WIPED DOWN the blade of her husband's sword with a clean, damp cloth. Sharp as a wicked tongue, the edge glinted in the sunlight as she raised it toward the sky. She slipped the sword back into the leather scabbard on the garden table and fastened her long, dark hair with a pin at her nape before she continued. A squirrel ran along the hedge on the left side of the plot. It continued across the grass and hopped up on the wooden fence on the right side. Turning its head, the critter seemed to eye Annarosa before he dashed up a tree trunk by the back wall. An encounter with nature in her own back yard. She smiled and picked up the second sword—her sword—and gently wiped the rag along the blade to remove any residue or dust. Then she propped the tip on a wooden block on the table for elevation. Applying even strokes to the sides of the blade with a whetstone, she allowed her mind to wander to when she and Claude had given their vows and moved into their lavish red home. Tall and with the depth of several rooms, the residence was indeed impressive. The Dutch government had dug three main canals and had built narrow row houses on the banks of these waterways to accommodate the growing number of well-to-do merchants in town. With her inheritance and Claude's employment as musketeer and emissary for King Louis XIII of France, they could easily afford such a lodging. Not that Annarosa needed luxury. As long as she could spend her life with Claude, she could live anywhere. In fact, her ultimate dream was a simple cottage by the woods, away from the commotion of Amsterdam.

Annarosa added some water and finished honing her sword as her lady's maid called her name from the doorway. The aged woman had been her chaperone for twelve summers now. Strict and meticulously observant, Simona was loyal and kind as few.

"Master Rembrandt is here."

"Thank you, Simona. Please show him into the garden."

Annarosa put the tools aside and turned to greet him. The man was in his mid-thirties but had youthful, round cheeks, curly brown hair that hung below his earlobes, and a friendly gaze. He must have come straight from his studio because the white ruff around his neck and the left sleeve of his coat had spots of yellow ochre paint. The small beard and mustache looked as if they had not been tended for a while.

Rembrandt grabbed his wide-brimmed hat, swung it in a circle, and bowed. "Annarosa, I'm delighted to see you." He kissed her outstretched hand.

"And good day to you. This is a pleasant surprise."

Pursing his lips, he passed a doubtful gaze. "A woman sharpening swords? An unusual sight, I must

53

say. But from what my friend Claude tells me, you're not only a devoted wife but quite the accomplished swordswoman."

Annarosa lowered her chin and smiled, then she looked up as he slowly picked up her sword.

"Careful, I just finished that one." She stretched her hand out to warn him. "That blade is deadly."

"Don't you have servants for this kind of work?" he asked.

"Oh, I never let anyone else touch our swords."

He thrusted it forward a couple of times. "What craftmanship. Perfect balance, leather-bound hilt for comfort, and an ornately engraved cross guard. There's even a jewel embedded there. Most fitting for a lady...if one thinks a lady should carry a sword." He put it gently back on the table, and his eyes crinkled at the corners. "I am jesting, dear Annarosa. The truth is, I'm in awe that such a beautiful woman can handle a weapon like this. I know a bit about swords—mostly from painting them—but would be struck down at first blow should I ever attempt to fight someone." He paused for a moment then added, "This is the one you brought with you when I painted your portrait, isn't it?"

"It is. Claude gave this to me when he started teaching me years ago. I know it will be with me for as long as I live. This piece of metal has already served its purpose and saved lives."

He cocked his head to the side. "You mean to say *you* saved lives?"

"Well, I did my utmost when my family was once ambushed by highwaymen, but there were three men against me. I was grateful beyond description when Claude showed up and chased the robbers away."

"Remarkable." Rembrandt lifted his chin. "Now, tell me. Where is that dashing musketeer friend of mine?"

"He was upstairs, wrestling with a squirrel, the last time I checked."

"What? A squirrel? Has he gone mad?"

Annarosa laughed. "Not at all. The animal jumped from a tree and into an open window on the other side of the house. Claude is trying to get it safely out again."

Rembrandt put his hands on his sides. "Ah, there's our Frenchman, now."

Claude strode toward them, smiling. He brushed his hands together. "Voilà. It finally hopped out the window and into the nearest tree."

Annarosa put her arm around his waist. "Oh, good. No harm done then."

Rembrandt raised his eyebrows. "And you have no injuries from this wrestling match either, I suppose?"

"Not a single one," Claude said, laughing. He picked up Annarosa's sword. "Excellent job, *ma belle*. Looks like you're about finished. Should we go inside? The breeze is picking up."

"You two go into the parlor. I'll be there soon." Once the men went inside, she carefully wiped off any excess metal shavings on the blade and slid her sword into the second scabbard. With both swords in her arms, she walked inside to join the others. A maid curtsied as Annarosa passed.

"Would you bring my tools on the garden table into the house? We may see some rain in a few moments."

The maid nodded and hurried off.

Annarosa found the men standing in front of a painted portrait of her madre.

"A portrait by the great Caravaggio," Rembrandt said,

rubbing the small bush of facial hair on his chin. "I have learned so much from the chiaroscuro technique he developed. What a treasure."

Annarosa smiled. "Yes, Madre said that of all the riches and Earthly possessions in her fine house, she valued two particular paintings the most—this one by Caravaggio and the Rubens portrait there with her and me. I've later come to understand that my madre had once been in love with Messer Caravaggio, but the two were never meant to be. Since he died, she looked for artists who followed in his footsteps." She turned to Rembrandt. "That's why she corresponded with you when we lived in Antwerp. She'd heard you were the most accomplished artist in Amsterdam."

Rembrandt placed the palm of his hand over his heart. "I thank you and your madre for such kind words. And now you have two of my works in your home." He pointed to the last two portraits in the parlor. "This one of you, Annarosa, and that one I painted earlier of my friend Claude in all his musketeer glory. I am honored that you both chose me to do these, and I wish your madre could have seen them."

"Please sit," Annarosa said. "Should I have the cook prepare something for us?"

Rembrandt wagged his finger. "No, no, I won't stay long. But thank you." A troubled look washed over his face, and he sat down on a soft chair propped with scarlet cushions tied with gold-colored tassels. "This brings me to why I wanted to see you today. It has come to my attention that a band of robbers specializing in stealing artwork has arrived in Amsterdam. I want to warn clients and friends of this worrying news. You know my house. Six rooms are devoted to art. My home could be a hunting ground for these thieves...and so could yours."

"Have you warned the councilors at the town hall and prepared the servants in your household?" Claude asked.

Rembrandt nodded. "I have. We take every precaution and hope for the best." He pushed himself up from the chair. "I must leave you now. My beloved Saskia is not feeling well."

"Then you should go home and tend to your sweet wife," Annarosa said. "When is the baby due?"

"Next month. We pray fervently the Lord will let us keep this one. Losing the first three children has left a heavy weight on my dearest...and on me." He put his hat on.

"We'll make sure to pay a visit soon," Claude said as he and Annarosa followed their friend to the front door and watched him head out into the rain.

FRIDAY, 27 APRIL 1945

CHAPTER SIX

OSLO, NORWAY

HER WORRIES FROM the day before undiminished, Soli walked about the shop, dusting frames on the wall and arranging the art history books on the table in the corner. She replaced a painting on the window display with a spring scene of mountains, a small cottage, and some cows. If Walter showed up, he'd probably find the nationalistic scenery perfect. She shuddered just thinking about him. Trying to please him was not her intent, but a rendition like that sold well during wartime.

Her thoughts returned to Heddy and the professor. Had they seen Walter coming? Had they gotten away, or had the lieutenant colonel taken them somewhere? And if the German officer had the painting now, would he take it back to Germany or give it as a gift to Minister President Quisling or Adolf Hitler?

As she was deep in thought, the notorious Lieutenant Colonel Heinz Walter entered the shop. As always, he had two of his men accompanying him.

Oh, yes, Walter was striking in his immaculate

uniform decorated with ribbon bars and aiguillettes. He still carried a dagger on his hip. Had he ever used it, or was it for show? Walter removed his visor cap as he strutted across the floor toward Soli. He propped the cap under his arm. The mane of dark hair was grayer at the temples than the last time she'd seen him, making him look all the more distinguished. Any woman would find him attractive, and he seemed to know it. His reputation as a flirtatious but demanding, high-ranking officer was firmly established. Unfortunately, she'd experienced his wolfish behavior the year before.

With a sharp click of his heels, Walter came to a halt in front of her.

"Good day, Miss Hansen. Or I suppose I should call you Soli. After all, we have been out together before, haven't we?"

How could she forget? The evening with him at a Nazi soirée at the Grand Hotel in Oslo had been far from comfortable. Fortunately, Soli had no problems under-standing his distinct German dialect. After five years of having to work alongside their occupants and studying their language in school, she'd become quite confident conversing. She curtsied.

"Good day. Welcome back."

She cringed as she said the words. Hopefully, he didn't notice her disgust with his presence in her store...in her home. In no way was he welcome. Not ever.

"I heard the previous owner died. Mr. Holm, was it?"

"Yes, he passed away last year. I take care of the shop now."

"You clever girl. I hope you have some male colleagues to lean on and speak to when you have questions. I'm sure you are overwhelmed by the responsibility."

She played along, smiling, nodding, pretending to be a naïve, young woman who couldn't think for herself. After his monologue about how difficult it must be to run a business as a single female, she eased in a question as he was drawing for breath.

"What can I help you with today? We have a beautiful painting on display in the window."

He grinned. "Yes, I noticed. Absolutely splendid. Not the stupidity of some of your modern artists like Munch." He strutted some more, stroking his finger along frames, and picking up a glass figurine on a pedestal, only to put it back in place. "I must say, my favorite pieces of art were painted by Flemish and Dutch masters centuries ago."

He had such a smug look on his face. *He has the Rembrandt.* Soli was certain of it. It was hard to concentrate. And what about Heddy and the professor? Had he interrogated them and forced them to reveal their secrets? Did he know about the other paintings in the Ruber collection by now?

Before she could ask him which of the master painters he enjoyed the most, the bell above the door jingled again. A man entered and waved one of Walter's men toward the door. They spoke low, then the man conveyed the message to Walter, speaking quietly into his ear.

Walter positioned his visor cap back on his head. "Well, Soli. I must run, but I'll come back another time. I have a personal matter I'd like to discuss with you."

He clicked his heels again then turned and left, his men following in his footsteps.

Soli sank into the soft chair in the corner. Why did he want to talk with her? Was he still interested in her as a woman? Did he need advice about art or perhaps want to talk about the Rembrandt she'd lost? Had her life been anywhere near normal she would have yelled no. No, she didn't want to see him again. No, she didn't want Walter or his men in her shop or anywhere near her...ever.

Soli rubbed her tightened fists in circles on her temples. Oh, what to do? She had absolutely no choice in the matter. If Walter knew where Heddy, the professor, and the musketeer painting were, Soli had to cooperate and spend more time with the lieutenant colonel.

* * *

As leader of their resistance unit, Heddy was the one who invited the others to meetings and coordinated what they needed to do. The boys respected her and would do anything from crossing through enemy territory to blowing up bridges for her. Now that she was missing, Soli took it upon herself to gather the group. They used to be a larger cell, but one of their friends had been arrested and shot, another had left, and Soli's brother Sverre had fled the country. Now, their Oslo unit consisted of the ever faithful and daring duo Birger and Arvid, Rolf who was their gifted planner, Soli's boyfriend Nikolai who worked as a detective at the police station at 19 Moller Street, Heddy, and herself. But with forty thousand men and women secretly fighting against their enemy, there were always crossover operations with other resistance groups. Working with such courageous people gave Soli a sense of belonging and a sharp awareness of the importance of battling for a cause greater than herself.

She locked up the shop at five and headed to Our Savior's Church. She passed the town square, but there were no vendors there now. Women still lined up outside the grocery stores early in the morning, hoping to apply their ration cards for a few items to feed their families. Printed on thick paper with the current authority's stamp and signature, the cards were hard to falsify and could only be used by the owner. Giving your cards to someone else or even selling them was illegal.

Soli's stomach growled just thinking about food. She hadn't eaten since breakfast, but since some of her ration cards were at the end of their three-week period, she had to be careful what she bought. She hadn't mentioned this to Nikolai the evening before. She figured he was hungry, too.

The iron gate on the right side of the church opened to a path that led toward the entrance of the crypt. This was where Heddy and her crew met under the pretense of being an art club. They even had drawing materials, watercolors, and brushes handy in case someone came uninvited. Soli was about to place a folded piece of paper in a slot in the brick wall when she heard rustling in the bushes behind the church. She noticed Birger's freckled face and broad smile first. That young man was always cheerful, a wonderful trait that often encouraged the rest of their group.

"Hello, Birger." Soli put her arms around him. Her heart ached when she felt how thin he was now. His clothes were several sizes too large for his frail limbs. Even his worn-out shoes looked as if they belonged to a bigger brother. But she didn't know anyone with more courage, despite his weak appearance. Just looking into those bright eyes and listening to his incurable optimism had lifted their spirits time and again.

Arvid stepped forward, removed his soft cap, and pushed his bushy blond hair back. Wearing knicker-bockers and a thick, knitted sweater, the man was the true image of an Arian warrior—tall, broad-shouldered, and strong as an ox. Together with Birger, Arvid had been Heddy's faithful helper since the war began. He grabbed Soli in one of his famous bear hugs and held her tight for a moment.

Soli chuckled low as he released her. "Hello, Arvid. How are you?"

"We're both fine. Right, Birger?" He put his hat back on and nudged his buddy.

"I was just leaving a message for you, knowing you check it every day in case Heddy needs to get hold of you."

Birger stood with his hands in his pockets. "And hocus-pocus! We're already here."

"That's much better." She turned her head left and right. Seemed like no one could see them there, a bit away from the street. "Come on, let's hurry downstairs. Too many ears and eyes out here."

She unlocked the heavy wooden door. The hinges creaked as Arvid pushed it open. He flipped a light switch inside and walked first down the stairs into the dimly lit, vaulted chamber. Old sarcophagi and gravestones stood among the stone pillars. To the left was a table and chairs.

"Come, sit down," Soli said.

Those boys meant the world to her. They fought for freedom and had given their all to help her safekeep paintings. Now she had to tell them Heddy had disappeared to Heaven knew where. She wasn't sure how to put it and wanted to make certain they didn't run off and start a rash search for their beloved leader and get arrested again.

"You probably wonder why I'm here and not Heddy."

"Not really. She's missing," Birger said and plopped down on a chair opposite Soli.

"How did you know?"

"We waited on the outskirts of town like Heddy asked us to. After a while, Nikolai showed up and told us what had happened. We spent the whole day yesterday and today looking for her."

"Yes, and several times a day, we came here and hid outside, keeping an eye on the entrance to the crypt in case she showed up."

Birger's big blue eyes had a seldom-before-seen, sorrowful look. "Where could she be, Soli? Heddy's never been away this long before. You don't think she's—?"

"No, Birger. We must believe she's alive and well. The question is, where?"

What else could she tell them? Soli had to convince both herself and these two brave men that their leader and friend would show up soon…unharmed.

"Now, boys. Let's gather our thoughts. I've a strong feeling the lieutenant colonel is behind her disappearance. We need to keep his moves around town under surveillance." Soli put a finger up, and with narrowed brows she added, "But mind you, he needs to be watched from a distance. I don't want you two in any trouble with him or his soldiers."

"Lieutenant Colonel Heinz Walter didn't manage to get rid of Birger and me the last time he had the Gestapo arrest us." Arvid tipped his head toward Birger. "Well, they kept our boy here a little longer." Arvid hit a tightened fist hard in his other hand. "If I had that Walter on my own, I'd—"

The young man leaned his arms on the table. "Yeah, they retained one of my teeth as a souvenir."

Soli offered a thoughtful expression. "You still have a wonderful smile, Birger, even with a tooth missing. But since they've seen your faces, all the more reason for both of you to stay out of their way." She took a deep breath and placed her folded hands in her lap. "Now, this is what I think. Walter came by my shop today, and I believe he'll be back to visit me very soon."

Arvid straightened up. "I don't like it. You're not safe alone with that brute, Soli."

"Well, I'm not so happy about the situation either. The lieutenant colonel is charming on the outside, but his actions are repulsive. If I'm to find out any information about what happened yesterday morning in Professor Holst's office, I need to step a little closer to Walter. Perhaps pretend I'm interested." She shuddered at the thought. "I don't think he knows my connection to any of you or even that Sverre is my brother."

Arvid slowly shook his head. "What does our detective friend think about this plan?"

"Oh, Nikolai doesn't know...not yet, but I doubt he'd approve."

"Is there any other way? It sounds dangerous," Birger asked.

Soli shrugged. "Aren't you the one who usually laughs at such a word?"

"Yes, but that's when my buddy here and I are in the front of the battle...not you or Heddy."

Arvid stood and started pacing around the room as he spoke. "I don't know about this, Soli. Toying with a German officer can be a deadly game."

Soli smiled. "You sound like my big brother, Sverre."

Arvid stopped wandering and gave her a solemn stare. "Sverre? Well, I take that as a compliment. But listen... you're a sister to us, as well, Soli. We'd do anything to keep you and Heddy safe."

"I know, and I'm so grateful." She paused for a

moment then asked, "Did Sverre ask you to watch over Heddy and me when he left the country?"

"Yes, but even if he hadn't, we still would've taken care of you girls."

"Well, thank you both. The best thing we can do now is to have a sound but flexible plan. Our first priority is to find Heddy and the professor. And I'd be so glad if we get our hands on the baroque painting, as well."

"How will we do this?"

"I'll receive Walter in a friendly manner when he returns to the shop, and you two should find out where he's staying then follow him and his men...but remember, do it from a good distance. One way or the other, we'll unearth where he's keeping our friends and the Rembrandt."

Arvid pulled a grimace. "Oh, we can do that, but you still shouldn't be alone with that man."

"Don't worry, boys. He comes during business hours, the shop is open, and customers will be coming in and out. Walter said he had a personal matter he wanted to discuss with me. I'm curious as to what it is." She gave the boys a comforting smile. "But I'll be careful...I promise."

SATURDAY, 28 APRIL 1945

CHAPTER SEVEN

OSLO, NORWAY

HALF AN HOUR after Soli had opened the shop the next morning, Walter and his two assistants marched through the door. They stopped in the middle of the showroom as if waiting for her to tread closer.

"Good morning," she said in German. "What can I help you with today?"

The lieutenant colonel had been there only yesterday, yet here he was again already. He removed his visor cap, placed it under his arm, and wandered about, picking up art history books from the display table, staring at the covers, and replacing them.

Trying not to sound presumptuous or overly eager, Soli tried again. She pointed to the wall covered with artwork for sale. "Do you see any paintings or drawings you prefer?"

"Hmm, you have a good eye for collecting pieces customers will buy." He turned sharply toward her. "That's why I'd like your input on a little place—a house, really—that I'm planning on moving into. I need a base here in Oslo and living in the Grand Hotel is becoming more tedious by the day. No, I'd much prefer to have my own home where I can entertain guests and, also, share with someone special."

Soli's blood seemed to freeze in her veins. What was he talking about? Walter had been interested in her before, but she was certain he'd given up the pursuit. She mustered all her strength to maintain a normal face and not panic. At least one piece of information was helpful— she now knew where he was staying.

"And what do you have in mind?" she asked, forcing her voice to remain calm and friendly.

He seated himself in the soft chair next to the table with art history books. "Well, you're an art historian extraordinaire. I'd think architectural history is also part of your knowledge."

"I've studied the various periods and styles."

"Exactly." He leaned back in the chair and stretched his long legs. "Now, I've found a place just a couple of streets from the royal palace. The whole area is elegant, but there's one villa in particular, a mansion that belonged to an avid art collector like me. The house has been unlived in for two and a half years—mice have chewed on the few things that are left there—and I need you to help me see what can be done to return both the exterior and interior to its former glory."

Soli didn't like where this was going. The Ruber residence was on Oscar Street. The building had stood empty since the deportation of the Jewish family, and no one had moved in or used it as offices. But it still wasn't owned by the Reich—not in her mind—and it certainly didn't belong to Walter. She'd never encourage him to move his belongings there. Her greatest hope for the place was for a living descendant of the Jewish family to take possession once the war had ended. And the conflict had to terminate one day. This spring they'd been more optimistic than ever before that Hitler's hours as dictator were numbered.

She gave a curt nod. "I'll see what I can do."

Walter rose from the chair and walked closer to Soli. "I'm gathering some quality art pieces these days. If you come across anything of interest, let me know, will you? So far, my trip this time has proven fruitful, but I'm sure there's more out there."

Soli nodded again, knowing she'd never divulge where the most valuable art was kept. Since the treasures from the National Art Gallery had been hidden just before the dawn of war, and other rescue missions to preserve artwork from Nazi looting were still going on, Walter had to work a little harder to find items of value. She studied his face. He had the musketeer portrait by Rembrandt in his possession—she was absolutely certain of it now. If he'd abducted Heddy and had forced her to reveal their secrets, Walter would be arresting Soli now, not telling her to help him locate art and provide restoration tips for an old mansion.

The lieutenant colonel placed his visor cap back on his head and clicked his heels. "That's settled then. Meet me at six outside the empty off-white mansion on Oscar Street. I don't remember the number, but it's the only one with pillars on either side of the entrance." He walked up to her, touched her chin, and winked. "Auf Wiedersehen, Soli."

In no way did she want to encourage his attention. "Goodbye," she said, her expression stoic.

Walter marched back out the door, followed by his two ever-present assistants.

Soli sank down on the floor. Alone with Heinz Walter and two German soldiers in an empty house? What was she thinking? Her stomach knotted. She had no choice. She couldn't say no to a high-ranking officer representing the Reich. Her only chance was to play along. If he knew where Heddy, the professor, and the Rembrandt were, then Soli would certainly try to get some information out of him.

Before meeting Walter, she had to go by the entrance to the crypt and leave a note for the boys. She'd feel much safer, knowing they'd come and hide somewhere across the street from the mansion, ready to rescue her should she need it.

Oh, how she wished Nikolai was here, holding her in his strong arms. On the other hand, he'd probably tell her not to go, that it wasn't safe.

Soli wiped her chin with a handkerchief from her pocket and threw it in the waste basket. Just thinking about Walter touching her sent a shiver up her spine.

An older man entered the shop, smiling.

"I'd like to buy a simple drawing," he said and removed his hat. "It's a gift. Nothing expensive please."

"Of course. Let me show you some examples."

Grateful she had work to keep her mind off her troubles, Soli asked the customer to sit down while she picked some suitable renditions. She still had a few hours before she had to meet Walter at Ruber's residence.

* * *

Soli checked her wristwatch as she turned the corner onto Oscar Street. *Ten minutes to six.* She slowed down and sauntered down the sidewalk. Had the boys found her note?

Were they hiding somewhere even now? If they'd already arrived, they were well hidden.

The thought that Walter had more than art on his mind troubled her. She'd certainly do her best to keep him at a distance and not encourage the man. What distractions could she use? Talk of art, delve into the history of renaissance painters, speak of how to blend colors for the best effect? She let her eyes wander toward hedgerows, brick walls, and fences, trying to spot Arvid and Birger. Hopefully, the boys were in the vicinity in case she needed help. Being around Walter was unbearable, not to mention dangerous. Besides, she had secrets of her own inside that house—cleverly hidden drawings and etchings by famous artist from the last centuries. That art also belonged to the Ruber family, and she'd do everything in her power to keep from saying the wrong words or behaving awkwardly and arousing suspicion. If she did, Walter might turn on her, tie her to a chair, and force the truth out of her.

Just thinking such thoughts made Soli's heart pound. She had to make sure it didn't go that far. The lieutenant colonel no doubt wanted to redecorate the place and keep the architectural details intact. Maybe even ask her for advice on what kind of art would look good in the rooms? She could do that. As long as he didn't ask her if she knew anything about where the Ruber family's legendary baroque art might have gone. He'd most likely heard rumors of such pieces. The trick was to encourage Walter do the talking so she could pick up clues about the Rembrandt portrait without divulging any of her own secrets.

Her watch showed a minute after six now. She'd better go and get this over with. She glanced a last time toward a cluster of trees across the street. Nothing. Where were those boys?

The rod iron gate squeaked as she pushed it open. A stone path went straight to the entrance of the impressive, two-story villa. Matching urns sat heavily next to the Dorian pillars by the door. It wasn't hard to understand why Walter found the mansion a perfect place to live during his visits to the Norwegian capital in the future.

Soli knocked once, and a smiling Heinz Walter brusquely opened the door. Was that a good sign? He was normally such a serious man. She stepped across the threshold, unbuttoned her jacket, then almost tripped as she saw who stood in the center of the hall.

Heddy.

Soli swallowed hard to compose herself. What was her dear friend doing there? Why was she with Walter, nicely dressed, and with a pleasant countenance on her beautiful face? Heddy was wearing a gray felt, cloche-style hat, not her usual beret. She also wore a burgundy-colored dress suit—she who usually always sported black trousers.

Walter made a gesture toward her friend. "Soli, this is Heddy. She's here to offer support and inspiration. If she likes this place as much as I do, we'll probably commence the renovation very soon." He smiled again and placed his arm around Heddy's shoulders.

We? What kind of relationship did he imagine he and Heddy had? Soli could just scream from frustration. Her head steamed with questions, but instead of spouting off the first thing that came to mind—such as, "What on Earth is going on here?"—she calmed herself, walked up to Heddy, and shook her hand.

"Good evening, I'm Soli Hansen. Very nice to meet you."

"Thank you for coming, Soli."

Heddy played the role of dutiful girlfriend to perfection. Or was she playing? Even Soli couldn't tell by her friend's facial expression what Heddy's thoughts were.

Soli was utterly confused now. She had to run her ideas down a different path, so she turned to Walter. "Should we get started?"

"Yes, this way, ladies." Walter led the way to the lounge.

Soli fervently glanced toward Heddy, trying to connect, but her friend didn't respond. She walked into the living room, her head held high, and stood next to the lieutenant colonel. This was going to be difficult. With no help from Heddy, Soli was on her own.

"Now, tell us about this home. I know it looks forsaken and dirty, and the wallpaper has faded, but it's been empty for a while. The family moved out...well, they were arrested. But luckily, this lovely building will soon return to the amazing edifice it once was, right Maus?" He nudged Heddy who answered with a sweet smile.

Maus? Goodness, this had gone too far. A German, high-ranking officer and a ruthless murderer was calling her best friend love names. Listening to him talking about common, everyday subjects left Soli with a peculiar feeling.

The empty room sounded hollow. Untended, shriveled-up plants sat in a silent parade of porcelain pots on the windowsill. The tall windows looked out on a back yard that must have been the scene for festive gatherings when the Ruber family lived here. Soli cleared her throat and stepped into the middle of the floor.

"This building was inspired by Italian Renaissance design. There's a lovely garden area in front, one that needs some work but that would give an imposing first impression when people come here. The façade toward the street is equally striking with the Dorian pillars and the upstairs veranda with French doors."

Walter had a smug look on his face as she spoke, as if he was proud of his home...a house that, in truth, didn't belong to him. He shoved his hands into his pockets. "I especially like the mullioned windows at the top of the front door."

Soli nodded. "Yes, they are pretty and in good shape, as well."

Walter started circling the floor. "What do you think about this room?"

"I believe new wallpaper and a bit of paint to the framework would be in order. The floorboards are still in fine condition. Other than that, I think it will look great once it's furnished again."

"And with some proper quality art on the walls, perhaps?"

There it was—the entrance to discussing art—her favorite subject...but not here, not now.

"Yes, a few well-chosen pieces would brighten the area," she answered curtly. "Should we continue to the next room?"

So far, so good. Walter showed them into the dining room. The women walked behind, but once again, there was no response when Soli tried to get Heddy's attention. She was utterly alone, even if her best friend was right there.

"Now, this dining area has a certain atmosphere," Walter said. "I can't quite put my finger on it, but it's as if it has been used for special occasions or that it's been a chamber for certain rituals...no, not rituals...perhaps for something secret, something the owner wanted to keep from the outside world."

Soli's muscles tensed, and she had to concentrate to breathe normally. Did the lieutenant colonel know about the clues on the wallpaper in the room and the art that had been hidden there? Or was he merely fishing for answers to rumors he'd heard?

Soli walked to the window. "There's a lovely view of the front yard and the street from here. A great room for entertaining dinner guests. You could fit quite a large table here in the middle, and perhaps a buffet over there against that wall.

"Hmm, perhaps." Walter strutted about with his hands on his back then stopped at the chimney and knocked on the whitewashed side with his knuckles. "Now, this is a riddle to me. Did you hear that? A hollow sound." He thumped on the chimney again. "I came by earlier and wondered why there was a pipe here but no fireplace or black iron stove." He placed a flat palm on the wallpaper and slid his hand across the surface. "Then there's this unusual pattern. A winged Mercury. Eccentric, isn't it?" He glanced at Soli. "You understand these things. What does it mean? Is there more to this place than meets the eye?"

Soli hated lying, but these were extreme times. War had made her do many things she wouldn't otherwise have done. Deceit had become a habit in order to survive. Yes, that room had special clues that had helped her find artwork the Ruber family had hidden from the Nazis. The chimney was a fake, and she certainly did not want to start a discussion with Walter about what it had been used for. She chose to satisfy his questions by offering her help.

"I really don't know. But I can look into it for you."

"You do that, Soli. If not, I'm sure I'll find out by some means."

They walked through the upstairs bedrooms, came down to the kitchen, then continued outside for a stroll around the yard. Walter seemed genuinely enthusiastic about the house and property. It was awkward to see him act this way.

Back in the hallway he asked, "So what do you think, ladies?"

Heddy adjusted her cloche hat. "It's very nice. I love it."

Finally, Heddy said something. She'd been awfully quiet during their tour of the manor, only nodding and smiling as if she agreed with everything Walter said. Soli had not acted any better, faking her encouraging remarks even if she didn't want the German officer there.

"How about you, Soli? Is this not a decent manor to represent our German ideals and to receive visiting dignitaries? I can fill it with art like the ones that used to grace these walls before."

How should Soli reply? *German ideals in a Jewish home in an occupied Norway.* What a ridiculous notion. Still, she needed to give him a proper reply. Walter was aware of some of the artwork, china, and jewelry the Ruber family had owned. Soli had seen him at an auction there the year before. He was waiting for her comment. His intense stare was uncomfortable enough to make her skin crawl. She would answer as well as she was able.

"Yes, this is a residential area behind the royal palace and a perfect location. With a little work and proper care, I agree this villa can be brought back to its former splendor."

"I'm glad to hear it. This could be the perfect place for me to stay when I visit Norway, especially now that I have someone special here to share this with."

He winked at Heddy, and she responded by tipping her head and smiling back at him.

Soli could just vomit. Heddy would never...in no way could Soli's friend seriously fall for the German officer. Her train of thought was abruptly broken when Walter asked the inevitable question.

"We both know the Jews who lived here had an extensive art collection. They had many fine things that didn't belong in the house of such people." He raised his finger. "And I've also heard rumors of an old book, sort of a Bible that explains about the art and where this family kept their treasures." Pressing his lips together, he kept a steady eye contact with Soli. "Do you know anything about such a book?"

The ledger. Soli had managed to keep him at bay thus far. She'd tried her best to dodge his comments with sensible answers and had even given him encouragement. But this question was so direct, so intense, Soli was terrified he'd notice her blank stare and that every muscle in her body had frozen. The sound of her heartbeat thrashed in her ears. Could he hear it?

Heddy stepped forward. "Could we not speak of this another time? The soirée at the hotel starts in twenty minutes."

He checked his watch. "Look at the time. I didn't realize it was this late. Thank you for reminding me, Maus." He resumed his stare at Soli, and his voice took on a stricter tone. "We'll continue this conversation later. If you know anything, I expect to hear every detail about that book. There may be more valuable pieces of art somewhere."

Walter started toward the door and looked back over his shoulder. "Come on, ladies. Time to go."

"It was a pleasure to meet you," Heddy said. Her handshake was firm with an extra squeeze as she stared Soli straight in the eyes.

Soli could have hugged her friend, laughed at the charade, but she gave a quick nod instead. "Farewell. Maybe we'll meet again."

Heddy smiled. "Yes, that would be nice."

Walter locked the door after them. Heddy followed him to a black car where his two men were waiting. At first, Soli had been elated once she realized the lieutenant colonel was interested in her merely as an art historian, not as a woman. More tormenting was the fact that, as he left, Heddy accompanied him. Her sweet friend was under the thumb of that brute. Yes, he'd been nice enough during the tour of the house, but Soli knew what he was capable of. That Walter had heard rumors about a ledger came as no surprise to her. She could kick herself when she thought about her reaction when he'd asked her if she knew anything about the old book. In the few paralyzing seconds afterward, a scene had played in her mind. She pictured him finding her secret room in the basement, taking the ledger she kept there, and forcing her to decipher the clues and riddles about the hidden art within its pages.

But there was hope. As she'd been numbly standing in the hallway, desperately hunting for the right words to say, Heddy had rescued her out of the compromising situation. That was the best thing about this whole evening—her friend was still on their side. Not that Soli had truly doubted her, but the uncomfortable circumstances had clouded her judgement.

As the car drove off, Soli's heart ached as if someone had stabbed her in the chest. What would happen to Heddy now?

Down the street, a group of soldiers were laughing. Soli buttoned her jacket and sighed. Fighting back the tears, she started for home.

CHAPTER EIGHT

SOLI TRUDGED INTO her room in the back of the store. She threw the keys and her shoulder bag on the table and kicked off her shoes. What had happened to Arvid and Birger? Why didn't they show up after Heddy and Walter had driven off?

Soli put the kettle on to boil some water for tea and had just sat down on the couch when someone knocked on the door. She froze. Two raps, then two more. Their safe knock. Relieved, she released a puff of air and went to answer.

"Nikolai." She flung her arms around his waist.

"Hello, you. That's quite a welcome."

"Please, hold me."

He tightened his grip around her, resting his head on hers, smelling her hair. "Rough day?"

"Uh-huh."

"It's been so busy at the station the last couple days. I'm sorry."

She treasured their openness with each other, but now

she held back. She hadn't warned him about her meeting with Walter. How would he react when she told him what she'd done?

Nikolai must have noticed her hesitation. "Do you want to talk about it?"

She took his hand and led him to the sofa. "Come sit."

"That bad, huh?" He put his trench coat and hat on the couch and plunked down next to her. "You know, one of my trusted men found out Walter is staying at the Grand Hotel. We've been following his movements, and this afternoon, we finally made some progress. But you first, Soli. Tell me about your day."

"Well, the lieutenant colonel came by the shop this morning—for the second day in a row."

Nikolai frowned. "He's up to something. What did he want?"

"He wants to take over Ruber's residence on Oscar Street and stay there whenever he's in Norway."

"What an opportunist. He must have pulled some strings to get permission to use that house?" He paused for a moment. "I'd think Walter would be reluctant about making plans right now. The war is going through a change. We received a message from London earlier today; the Italian fascist dictator Benito Mussolini was executed by a partisan group. There's hope, Soli."

"I pray you're right about that. In the meantime, Walter believes in a future where he'll still order us around. He wants me to give him advice on restoring the property and to suggest suitable artwork."

Nikolai jerked back. "No, I don't want you to even think about going there by yourself."

"I already did."

He sat up straight. "You went on your own with that

man to an empty house? Soli, why? With everything that's happened, Walter is extremely dangerous."

Soli sighed. She'd taken a terrible risk. "As it turned out, I wasn't alone with him. Heddy was there. I'm more worried about her."

"Heddy?" He shook his head. "Oh, this is getting worse. That's what I was going to tell you. My assistant sighted a beautiful, dark-haired woman with Walter. From the description, I knew it had to be Heddy." Nikolai ran his fingers through his hair. "I understood from my man's report that she had befriended the lieutenant colonel in some sort of way, but I had no idea she spent that much time with him."

"Walter behaved as if they were a pair, and Heddy played the role perfectly. I didn't get to talk to her, but before she left with him, I had the impression she knew what she was doing." Soli stroked his cheek. "I took precautions and asked Arvid and Birger to keep watch outside the building...although, I never saw them."

He relaxed his shoulders. "Good. The boys were probably there somewhere. Did he force her along, or has she voluntarily gone with him to spy on him to acquire information about the professor and the painting?"

"I'm not sure. Heddy didn't speak to me or share eye contact. She kept her distance, except for the one time she squeezed my hand as we said goodbye."

"The lieutenant colonel could have abducted her and the professor, or she's pretending to be on his side."

"I worry about her. She's always taught me how to stay safe. It's hard to understand that a woman who's scarcely slept in the same apartment for several days in a row the last five years would choose to spend her time with a

German officer like Heinz Walter. The thought is unbearable."

Nikolai put his arm around Soli's shoulders and pulled her close. "Heddy is smart and careful. She always plans every operation in detail."

"I know, but she may not have had much time to plan. She came to the professor's office to meet me and get the painting. What happened there before you and I arrived?" Soli shook her head. "One thing I know for certain is that Heddy would never betray us or our beloved country. But I'm terrified something bad will happen to her. Arvid and Birger are also beyond themselves with worry."

There was another rap on the back door.

"Speaking of the boys… That must be them." Nikolai rose to his feet and went to answer.

"Good evening, Detective," Arvid said.

Birger followed his tall mate inside and nodded to Soli and Nikolai as he crossed the threshold.

"Here, sit on the couch next to Soli." Nikolai moved his coat and hat out of the way.

"What happened to you two?" Soli said. "I know you are experts at hiding, but where were you?"

Arvid sat slumped, twisting his hands in his lap. "When we turned onto Oscar Street at a quarter to six, we saw a Gestapo vehicle drive up and stop outside the Ruber's residence. And then we—"

"We saw our Heddy!" Birger blurted out. "She walked inside with the lieutenant colonel."

Birger scratched his chin. "There were a couple of uniformed men still in the car, so we hurried around the other way, taking some back streets, and ended up on the opposite side a little farther from the gate."

Nikolai grabbed a stool and sat down, facing them. "I

understand. You couldn't exactly walk into the arms of the German secret police."

Arvid nodded. "No, they were too close."

Birger lifted his eyebrows. "But we saw you coming, Soli, and we stayed close until you and Heddy had both left. Then we ran off in the other direction as there were other groups of soldiers in the area."

Soli put her hand on Birger's arm. "Thank you for being there for both Heddy and me. You are such wonderful friends."

Nikolai gave a crisp nod in agreement. "Soli was just telling me about what happened."

Arvid and Birger were eager to know everything. Soli gave a detailed explanation about her visit to Ruber's residence. With concentrated gazes, Nikolai and the boys listened intently without interruptions.

Nikolai finally spoke up. "Now what? We know Heddy spends a lot of time with Heinz Walter but not where she's staying. And we still have no knowledge of Professor Holst's whereabouts. Also, if Walter took the Rembrandt, where is he keeping it?"

Soli got up from the couch and resolutely put her hands on her hips. "We need to go back to Oscar Street."

Arvid, who was brave but ever cautious, said, "Walter could return at any time—day or evening."

"Yes, that's true. But we must remove the rest of the hidden artwork from the premises before he finds them."

"Not tonight, Soli," Nikolai said. "It's Saturday evening, and the town is swarming with soldiers. I suggest we go tomorrow. The streets are usually much quieter on Sundays."

Arvid sat up. "We're in."

Birger followed the conversation with rapt attention,

always willing and eager to help a good cause. Suddenly, he stood and opened his jacket. From large inside pockets on both sides, he pulled out two loaves of bread. "I almost forgot. We stopped by the bakery where my aunt works on the way here. Even on a Saturday evening, she was there working and had just delivered freshly baked goods to a party at the Grand Hotel. She'd saved a couple and gave them to me. Where's your cutting board and knife, Soli?"

"You can use this tray, and the knife is in that first drawer," Soli said. "Mm, they smell delicious."

"Yes, I was afraid someone would notice the scent as we hurried here. People are dead tired of bark and potato breads."

"As are we," Nikolai said. "But it fills the stomach." He turned to Soli. "Do you per chance have anything else we could add to this feast?"

"I have lingonberry jam, syrup, and canned herring." She placed the items on the table. "And how about I make some pea coffee?"

Nikolai smiled. "Perfect."

They sat down, happy to have a meal together but, at the same time, Soli was sad Heddy was not there with them. Soli gazed into each of their faces. They were good men, brave and loyal. She had to believe they'd be able to rescue Heddy from Walter's grasp.

There was another knock. Not on the back door but a distant rap.

"There's someone at the shop entrance," Nikolai said. "You boys stay here. I'll go with Soli and see who it is."

CHAPTER NINE

NUME VALLEY, NORWAY

THE ENTRANCE TO the shop had been closed since early afternoon. It was Saturday, after all. Soli stood back for a moment, observing the door. Then she swallowed hard and strode across the showroom to answer the knock. Who on Earth would come knocking at such an hour? Her friends would have walked around the building to the back. Was it safe to open? She glanced back at Nikolai, and he nodded.

"Go ahead, Soli," he whispered. "I'm right here."

Her brave detective remained off to the side, hand on his pistol, ready to jump forward. Soli pushed the shade that covered the glazing and peered out. A young woman stood on the front step. She looked barely twenty and wore a knitted cardigan over a black dress with a white collar. Comfortable leather shoes told Soli the girl was not on her way to an evening on the town. Most likely, she came straight from work.

Soli opened the door. "May I help you?"

The maid handed her a piece of paper folded in two.

"The pretty, dark-haired woman in room 302 at the Grand Hotel asked me to give you this."

"What's her name?"

The maid shrugged. "I try not to get involved with our guests, but she requested my help." She curtsied and turned to leave.

Soli touched her arm. "Wait. Please tell me, is she well?"

Looking left and right then taking a step forward, the maid spoke in a low tone. "I think she's in a bit of trouble. The German officer has someone watch her every move. I see them patrolling the floor where her room is, and she had me deliver this in secrecy without them knowing." She took a quick look over her shoulder. "I hope they didn't follow me here."

Soli stretched her neck. "There's no one there—at least, not that I can see—but you should hurry home."

The maid buttoned the top pewter button on her cardigan and looked up at the dark-gray sky. "Good Saturday to you."

"And to you." Soli put her hand on the woman's arm. "Thank you. That was brave what you just did."

The young woman smiled then turned and ran across the street.

After locking the door, Soli walked back to Nikolai while opening the note.

"It's from Heddy."

He widened his eyes. "Oh, finally. Come, read it in the other room with the boys."

Arvid and Birger met them halfway.

"We heard," Arvid said. "Read the message, Soli."

Let's have blueberries at mid-day tomorrow.

Birger put his hands out. "What? How do you know when and where to meet?"

"I know precisely what Heddy means, and I'll be there."

Birger couldn't hold his eagerness inside. He gave Soli a big hug. "Can we come?"

Arvid nudged his arm. "She may not be alone, my friend. But we should follow Soli there and stay in the vicinity."

Birger grinned. "All right. I can't wait to see if Heddy's all right."

Nikolai cupped Birger's shoulder. "We should all go. But for now, let's finish the delicious bread, and Soli can explain more."

* * *

Heddy sat at a corner table in the smoke-filled rococo hall of the Grand Hotel. She'd never been there before, but Soli had told Heddy about the splendor of the finest banquet room in Oslo. The mirrors on the left wall reflected the evening light from the tall windows facing the street. Sparkly crystal chandeliers hung from the gilded stucco on the ceiling. Soli must have enjoyed observing the elaborate murals when she was there last. The paintings depicted angels with billowy capes and horses floating on clouds.

Heddy wrung her hands in her lap. She'd started a farce—a horrid charade of pretending to enjoy Walter's presence—and she had to finish it. But tonight, she'd taken a great risk just before Walter had come to pick her up. Not being able to talk with Soli and explain why she'd ignored her at the Ruber residence, Heddy had involved an innocent maid to help deliver a message. Most of all, Heddy had wanted to hug Soli at the residence and whisper in her ear that they should run out the door together. But with Walter there, it had been impossible. So, when she'd seen the maid in her hallway on the third floor, holding a knitted cardigan in her hand and ready to go home after a long day's work, Heddy had jumped at the chance. She'd made a spur-of-the-moment decision— totally lunatic with the German soldiers patrolling her floor and even riskier if the girl had been pro-Nazi.

"Would you come to my room for just a minute... please? The curtains won't close properly, and I've tried everything," she'd said to the maid.

The girl had peered toward Walter's men by the staircase but had then followed Heddy into her room.

Heddy had quickly closed the door, torn a sheet of paper from a notepad on her nightstand, and written down a few words. She'd folded it in half and had handed it to the girl.

Leaning close, Heddy had whispered, "Please take this note to Holm's Art Shop by the town hall and give it to Soli Hansen. No one else." She'd placed a bar of chocolate into the maid's hand, a rare treat these days, but one of the privileges of spending time with Walter. The young woman had gratefully slipped the chocolate and the note into her purse.

Heddy had stood in her doorway, watching the girl patter down the hall. When one of the men had put his arm out in front of the maid and demanded to know what she'd done in Heddy's room, the girl had explained with a giggle how some hotel guests needed help with every-

HEIDI ELJARBO

thing. The men had snickered, mumbling something
about dizzy-headed females.

When the maid had disappeared down the back stairs.
Heddy had run to the window. A minute or two later,
she'd caught sight of the girl on the sidewalk, strolling in
the direction of Soli's art shop.

The angels with the billowy capes seemed to smile
down from the ceiling. Heddy lowered her gaze to where
Walter stood talking with a group of officers. He threw his
head back, laughing so loudly she could hear him above
the music and noise in the room. How could she be a spy
who mingled with the likes of the lieutenant colonel?
Who would have thought? Not her. Heddy had no ambi-
tion to be anywhere near German soldiers. Why would
she? She had Sverre. Soli's brother had captured Heddy's
heart the first time they'd met. Memories of that day were
unforgettable and dear. It was the day after their country
had been invaded. Heddy had sat on the sofa in her friend
Rolf's apartment with other volunteers willing to fight the
intruders. Then Sverre had entered and looked straight at
her. His thick blond mane paired with determined blue
eyes were still to die for, but more than that, it was his
fighting spirit, the unwavering sense of righteousness, and
his brave nature that made him irresistible.

Rolf had been quick to introduce them. Rolf, her intel-
ligent, clever co-partner in their resistance unit. His
health was failing now, and even though Heddy often
went by his apartment to ask for advice or help, she made
sure he didn't need to physically take part in their clandestine operations.

Walter was a man devoid of empathy and compassion.
How was that even possible? How could a person trample
another down without remorse? No, Heddy was forever

grateful she'd found someone who didn't exploit others but rather encouraged and lifted them up above himself. Had it been love at first sight? For her, yes, and it hadn't taken long before Sverre had confessed the same feelings for her.

Oh, that her love was safe now. She had not seen Sverre since she and the boys had helped him across the border to Sweden. He was well known by the Gestapo and other resistance hunters. Sverre had been beaten and bloody, and they'd had no other option but to make him disappear for a time. Not that he sat idly in Stockholm, waiting to return to Oslo. Undercover work and distributing information from their main leaders in the London office could be accomplished from the Swedish capital. All Heddy wished for was a life of freedom spent alongside that good man.

She lifted her gaze to Walter again. Oh, no. He was obviously done talking and strode toward her, a grin on his face.

"Care to dance, Fräulein?"

She forced a smile, took his outstretched hand, and let him lead her into the middle of the floor. The room was crowded and the music too loud for a decent conversation. Unfortunately, the energetic jazz compositions and entertainment tunes used as an escapism from the soldiers' otherwise strict routines of military and classical music now faded. Instead, the bandleader had the violinist play a mellow melody. The lieutenant colonel pulled Heddy close. His warm hands, the smell of hair tonic, and his tobacco-breath made her nauseous. Not necessarily the scents, but because he was Heinz Walter. Heddy wished she could simply disappear like the girl in a children's story about Dorothy and the Wizard of Oz her mother had told her many years ago. When Dorothy's troubles became unbearable and she wanted to escape back home, she'd clicked her heels and disappeared to a different place. Heddy was wearing her red pumps. Still, no such luck for her. She had to brave the hurricane and try her best to complete her mission. Where had they taken Holst? She had yet to hear Walter mention the professor. And what was his plan for the Rembrandt portrait? So far, she only knew the kind, old man had vanished, and she was pretty sure the crate with the painting was in Walter's hotel room on the second floor. He'd mentioned it when they'd discussed art on their way back from Oscar Street.

Walter guided her along to the rhythm, crisscrossing between the other couples and even dipping her a couple of times. There was nothing wrong with his dancing skills. In fact, the lieutenant colonel was quite the accomplished dancer. It was the company she didn't care for. Heddy floated past other women who, contrary to her repulsion, seemed thrilled about a night out.

As the song ended, Walter checked his watch. "Ah, it's late. Should we retire to my room? I'll have the waiter bring us something delicious to drink, and we can—"

Heddy put a finger to his lips. "Please, not tonight. I have the most dreadful headache." She made a pinched expression, closed her eyes, and slowly opened them again.

"Hmm, well, how about you go take a pill for your pain and come back downstairs? Surely, you have something like that in your purse."

"I have a pillbox with *Globoid* in my room, but I'm afraid those alone don't help much. A dark chamber and quiet is what I need. Thank you for a divine evening. Please excuse me."

He kissed her hand, and she turned and left. She wasn't worried about his feelings. The man was married. Heddy had seen a photograph of a woman standing next to three young children one time he'd flipped his wallet open in the hotel lobby. She'd also heard Walter ask his men to pick up a gift for his wife to take back to Germany. Somebody else would no doubt come along and keep him company for the rest of the evening. There were plenty of attractive women in the room who cast long glances at the distinguished officer.

Oh, what had she done? She was not an actress. How could she keep up a charade with a man she found utterly revolting?

Heddy had been able to ward off Walter's advances so far. She could do it forever. He would never get under her skin, no matter how gallant he behaved when he treated her to dinner and sent her flowers. There was nothing chivalrous about the man. Walter simply stepped on corpses to get his way.

Climbing the stairs to her floor, Heddy shook her head. Divine? Could she not have used a different word to describe the evening with him? It didn't matter now. She'd managed to escape, but how long would she be able to keep her distance from him? She had to find out where the professor was before she could execute her flight. At the top of the stairs, she turned to check if anyone followed her. No, not yet. If she hurried, she might be able to pick up her things and leave through a back door. Tempting, but how would she acquire the information she needed if she walked away now?

Her thoughts went to the young maid. Such a risk for the young woman, but Heddy had no choice. With no telephone in her room, she couldn't communicate with her friends. If she went to the front desk to make a call, Walter's men would be close enough to follow the conversation. They'd probably even listen in. The hotel staff might not be trustworthy either.

Desperate to talk to Soli, Heddy still held her head high as she entered the hallway on the third floor. How she longed to explain why she was with Walter, why she'd behaved the way she did, and let everyone know she was safe...at least, for now.

The familiar German voices of Walter's men sounded behind her. Heddy rolled her eyes. That brute had once again sent his men to control her movements. One thing she knew for certain, he did not trust her.

~ CAPITOLO III ~

AMSTERDAM, HOLLAND
MID-AUGUST 1641

ANNAROSA AND CLAUDE stood outside Rembrandt's magnificent row house in the southern section of *Sint Antoniesbreestraat*. The local community consisted mostly of merchants, many of them Jewish, and the master painter enjoyed trailing the streets to study people's faces for his biblical scenes. The area was also crowded with wealthy patrons of art, something that attracted painters.

"I remember well the first time we went here together," Claude said and fastened his grip around Annarosa's waist. "You came to have your portrait done, and I followed you like an enamored puppy."

"We were both too polite to admit our feelings at the time," she said with a smile. "I'm so grateful we both felt the same way." She raised her chin and gazed up at the three floors above the basement. The house, although narrow, had the width of four large windows. Whispering, she leaned close. "This must have cost Rembrandt a fortune."

"Indeed. He bought this place two years ago. He has

had formidable success and thought this suited his ambitions."

A servant opened the door and led them into a high-ceilinged hall with a tiled floor.

Claude let Annarosa go first. "This room is where he receives patrons and business relations. The antechamber through there is where people usually sit and wait to be seen."

The servant bid them take a seat in the antechamber but soon returned.

"Madam would like to see the lady in her salon, and Master Rembrandt will receive you, sir, upstairs in his studio."

"Très bien," Claude said. "Very good. Come, Annarosa, I'll take you to the back room." In a dark hallway, he pointed to a door straight ahead, blew her a kiss, and climbed the stairs.

Annarosa knocked on the door farthest back in the house. To be invited to the family's salon was quite personal. This was where Rembrandt and his wife ate, slept, and lived together.

"Come in," a frail voice sounded from inside, followed by a hacking cough.

Without hesitation, Annarosa entered the spacious chamber. Light streamed from windows high up on the left wall, and a spectacular fireplace dominated the right side.

"I'm over here, dear. Please pull up a chair and sit with me."

Annarosa turned to find Saskia propped up among pillows and blankets. The built-in bedstead had curtains on the sides, and the wooden structure was richly carved. Annarosa pushed a chair close to the bed and sat down.

Even with Saskia's health on the line, they had an agreeable conversation, speaking of household duties, the pleasures of living in a thriving town like Amsterdam, and how to prepare for the birth of Saskia's child in a few weeks. Her eyes glowing with intelligence and humor, Saskia seemed spirited and fearless in her opinions yet gentle when she mentioned servants or neighbors.

Curious about how Saskia had come to marry Rembrandt, Annarosa had to ask. "You have told me how you lost your parents at an early age and how your sister raised you. Still, you were educated and spent time with intellectuals. I apologize for asking, but you and your husband seem such a compatible and harmonious couple. I suppose it was not an arranged marriage. After all, you wedded the most famous painter in Amsterdam. How did you two find each other?"

Saskia's small, round lips curled upward. "I was privileged to grow up with a father who was the mayor and justice of the court of Friesland. When he died, I was only twelve years old, but he left us status and money. I was not the kind of woman who married the first man who came along. My uncle Hendrick Uylenburgh lived next door to our home here. He had a studio with various young artists, and my Rembrandt headed his atelier. I spent much time there, watching the artists paint portraits for the new residents of Amsterdam and their families. Even though he was the son of a miller with a considerably less affluent background than mine, we shared a passion for life and art. He was so different from the other painters. My Rembrandt creates stories through his work." She moved toward the edge of the bed, her protruding stomach showing through the linen smock. "Come, help me up. I spend too much time among these pillows. Let me accompany you upstairs to the studio."

With Annarosa supporting her back Saskia swung her legs out, sat on the side of the bedstead, and slipped her feet into the house shoes on the floor.

A flowing golden gown with several skirts and a boned bodice hung across the back of a chair. It would look lovely against Saskia's strawberry-blonde hair.

She caught Annarosa looking at the clothes. "No, just hand me the maternity robe on the hook over there. It's simple, but I don't need to dress up today." She coughed into a handkerchief, leaving a small spot of red on the cotton material. "I can't bear the whalebone stomacher against my chest today."

Annarosa helped her friend into the woolen bodice with an attached red skirt and tied the ribbon in front. She covered Saskia's chest with the linen partlet and pinned it into place. Annarosa then added the natural beige waist-coat, fastening the brass hooks at Saskia's chest.

Saskia gave her a grateful smile. "And my coif, please. My hair is such a mess today."

It was a shame to hide Saskia's golden curls under a close-fitting bonnet—it made the young woman look even paler—but Annarosa did as she was told.

Arm in arm, they walked up the stairs and into the studio. Annarosa strolled slowly past the many pen and ink drawings of Rembrandt's sweet wife, artistic rendi-tions of how much he adored her; Saskia having her hair brushed, sleeping, looking out a window, staring at her husband in an alluring way. In some sketches her hair was tousled; in others she had pearls in her tresses and gems dangling from her ears.

Rembrandt bowed to Annarosa then pulled out a chair

for his wife. "Here, my dearest. You look wonderful today."

Claude approached the woman and kissed her hand. "Good day, Saskia. We're discussing the change in the art world from religious and mythological motifs to portraits of people. What do you think?"

Saskia placed a pensive hand on her cheek. "Oh, my dear. We live surrounded by art. We have nine rooms in this house. As you probably know, six of these are dedicated to my husband's work. Students work on the top floor, and buyers frequent the hall downstairs. His assistants run in and out of this studio at all times of day. For us, it's a way of life but a good one. If people want their portraits painted by my Rembrandt, I am proud and pleased."

Rembrandt walked over to Annarosa and whispered, "How do you find her today?"

"We've had the most pleasant conversation. There's nothing wrong with her wit and cleverness."

His lips were tightly drawn. "She's been mine for nearly eight years, and I cannot bear the thought of losing her."

Annarosa placed her hand on his arms and gave it a gentle squeeze. "Try not to worry. The coughing tires her but so does the child she's carrying. We all pray for a healthy baby and that Saskia will regain her strength again. You must have hope and faith."

"Hope and faith. Yes, those two words go together, don't they?"

She nodded. "They do. Don't give up."

Rembrandt straightened his back. "Will you take supper with us? I'm starving."

"I'm afraid we must decline," Claude said. "Our old

maid, Simona, has been alone for a few hours since we gave our servants the afternoon and evening free. She's afraid of the dark, and we should return home now."

Rembrandt gave a curt nod. "Oh, the loyal Simona. Of course, you should go."

Annarosa took Saskia's outstretched hand in both of hers. "We bid you farewell, but we'll come again. Meanwhile, you must take care of yourself and the child in your womb."

Saskia gave her a tired smile. "Until then."

* * *

They hired a carriage to take them home. Darkness was falling, and a full moon shone on the water in the canals. A lamplighter was up ahead, holding a long pole to light the candles in the lanterns on the bridge. They passed more of these workers on the way, men who lit and maintained the lamps outside inns and taverns. When the carriage stopped outside their gate, Claude stepped out and gave Annarosa his hand to help her.

As he paid the driver, she gazed toward the house. "Why are there no lights in our windows? Simona would not have retired to bed this early."

Claude took her hand. "Perhaps she was especially tired tonight."

A dissatisfied frown formed on her face. Something was wrong.

Claude put an arm around her shoulders. "Come, let's find out."

As they approached the house, they heard noises from the parlor. Silent as the early morning prayers in a cloister, Annarosa unlocked the front door, and Claude soundlessly stepped inside and found their swords in the salon. They moved softly toward the parlor, trying to avoid the parts where the floorboards creaked. The person must have heard the swish of their swords scraping against the scabbard as they pulled them out because as soon as they reached the parlor, he ran out the door and into the garden. They followed him out and onto the lawn.

The man turned and jerked a rapier from the sheath hanging from his belt. He had chin-length black hair with a few strands that partly covered one eye. A rather limp blue hat was pulled far down over his head, giving him the impression of an individual who did not follow fashion trends but went his own way.

"En garde," the man said and positioned himself in a defensive stance.

Claude and Annarosa moved to either side of the man, preparing to be attacked or ready to bout, whatever came first.

"A female...what is she doing here?" The man spoke with a foreign accent. Polish, perhaps, or even from one of the countries farther south.

"I'm not going anywhere," Annarosa said. "You entered our home uninvited."

The thief looked at Claude then moved his gaze to Annarosa, clearly confused at her presence. He drew a dagger from his left hip and swung both weapons in rapid circles, frantically moving his eyes back and forth between his opponents.

Claude said sternly, "You heard the lady. Now, will you surrender?"

Baring his teeth, the man shouted. "I will not."

Despite his brave words, the intruder displayed a frantic expression of being overwhelmed. Would he run around the corner to hide or continue? After they'd let him breathe for a few seconds, he shoved the dagger back into the sheath and brought the rapier forward with a furious thrust. They could kill him easily—but that was never the purpose. Annarosa tightened her grip around the hilt of her sword, holding it ready in case she needed to defend herself. The man swung at Claude, and her husband parried the thrust with ease. Attacking again, the man advanced, aiming at Claude's throat, but Annarosa swung her sword around and up, splitting open the man's coat across his ribcage. He cried out, held his left arm across his breastbone for a moment, then positioned himself for another blow.

It was merely a flesh-wound. Annarosa had no regrets. Claude had taught her to defend and attack when needed. Even though the thief moved as one who had been trained well, she had no doubt her beloved could guard himself. But here and now, she would do everything to assist him and protect their home.

A clamor from inside the house caught her attention. It sounded as if someone was kicking a door. *Simona.*

Claude had heard it, as well. "Go. Take care of her," he said between blows. "I can handle this scoundrel."

Annarosa ran inside. Whimpering sounds came from the pantry. She put her sword on the side table, pushed a chair out of the way, and opened the door. Simona was on the floor, a gag stuffed in her mouth and her hands tied at her back. Annarosa helped her chaperone into a standing position and pulled the cloth out of her mouth. After untying the rope around Simona's wrists, Annarosa gently embraced the old woman.

"Oh, my dearest Simona. What has he done to you? Are you hurt?"

The old maid shook her head. "I kicked the door and tried to make as much noise as possible."

"You did well. I'm proud of you."

Simona started sobbing.

Annarosa gently wiped the tears and stroked her cheek. "There...there."

"But Annarosa, he came for the paintings."

Annarosa's jaw dropped, and she ran into the parlor. She lit a candle and held it up. Caravaggio's portrait of her madre was there, so was the one Rubens painted of Madre and Annarosa as a little girl. Also, the painting their friend Rembrandt had rendered of Annarosa, seated and with the sword across her lap. But as she looked for the fourth portrait, her eyes moistened with tears. The space on the wall where the precious painting of Claude had hung was empty.

Startled, as someone entered the door to the garden, she spun around. Pressing a palm to her heart, she let out an elated sigh. "Oh, Claude. You're back. Did you get him?"

"Yes and no. We fought for a while. The man has the skills of a military swordsman but presented a rather rough execution."

"Yes, I noticed that. But where is he now?"

"He seized a knife from his left boot and hurled it at me. As I ducked, he escaped through the gate in the back wall. I followed and saw two other men on horseback waiting for him. He mounted a third steed, and they rode off, dust whirling up as the horses galloped the street northward. Fortunately, we have a lantern next to our gate. It gave enough light for me to notice that the horses wore the same saddle blankets. The covers had the mark of the tavern opposite the guild hall. Either the men have stolen those animals, or they work for the innkeeper. I'll go straight away to see if I can find them."

Annarosa gave him a pained look. "They have your Rembrandt."

Claude scowled. "Well, they won't get far. Stay here with Simona." He kissed Annarosa's cheek then cupped Simona's shoulder in his strong hand before he turned and left.

SUNDAY, 29 APRIL 1945

CHAPTER TEN

OSLO, NORWAY

HEDDY LAY CURLED under the eiderdown cover. Nightmares had kept her awake most of the night, and she'd finally been able to find sound sleep for the last few hours. She climbed out of bed and looked out the window of her room at the Grand Hotel. Morning light bathed Karl Johan Street, presenting a quieter scene than the evening before. She'd rarely heard so much noise on a Saturday night in the capital. It was as if people were making the most out of their last days on Earth.

The war was finally at a breaking point. She'd listened in on some of Walter's discussions with his men. Underneath their blatant, loud words touting victory and glory —even if they'd been brainwashed to believe they were a superior race—surely, they had to understand their Führer was losing his grip. The men had spoken of a future with total white supremacy, a world wherein the Reich was completely in charge. Watching their faces, Heddy had sensed that despite their arrogance and boastfulness, the fear of defeat and retaliation weighed heavily on their minds. Well, perhaps not all of them. The lieutenant colonel appeared haughty as ever.

Hopefully, the maid had been able to deliver the note to Soli. Only Soli would be able to understand the cryptic message. Heddy was more worried about how to steer clear of the two men assigned to keep an eye on her. She only needed a few minutes—a short while to give Soli a hug, explain the situation, and tell her friend everything was under control. Did she have everything under control? No, it certainly didn't feel like it. She was moving forward one small step at a time, trying to get the information she needed. Without that goal, she would have escaped already. It was totally ridiculous. Why did Walter keep her under surveillance? It was as if he was fascinated with her, but nonetheless, suspicious of her every movement. How sad to live such a paranoid life, always on guard. But didn't she live in a similar manner? Hadn't she been looking over her shoulder each day for the last five years? She was skeptical of the whole world except her small group of trustworthy friends. Everyone else she kept at a distance, apprehensive about which side they were on in this horrid war.

Even with all the clandestine operations Heddy had taken part in, she'd always kept a low profile. That Walter surveilled her actions to see if she had a dubious background was understandable. He probably did so with every person he spent time with. Hopefully, he hadn't found any steadfast evidence of who she really was. The thought that she'd be able to disappear if she chose to do so was the only thing that kept her going. She had carefully planned two different escape scenarios with details like the time of day, how to avoid the guards, and how to vanish like a ghost once she was out on the street. Oslo was her town, and her strength lay in knowing every alley, building, and park.

No matter how tempting such a flight was, she sighed, knowing she had to wait just a bit longer in hopes of finding out what Walter's plans were for the professor and the Rembrandt painting. A strong feeling of running out of time overwhelmed her as she got dressed. After she met Soli, she'd make a bolder move and try to retrieve information from Walter. Even if she had to... No, she couldn't bear the thought of flirting with him. He'd kissed her twice, and she could barely contain how disgusted she was. Hollywood would surely give her a medal for her merits and acting abilities.

A pitcher of water and a ceramic bowl stood on a side table. She wiped her face with a washcloth and gave her hair a good brushing. Her black trousers hung across the back of a chair—her preferred outfit—but she'd better keep up the appearance of an elegant woman. She donned the burgundy-colored dress suit and was adding the last touches of red to her lips when someone rapped on her hotel door.

"Coming." She grabbed her jacket and purse and went to the door.

Walter stood in the hallway, his uniform in perfect order, and his visor cap tucked under his arm.

"Good morning. Sleep well?" He didn't pause for her to answer but continued. "I thought we could have breakfast together. You're not working today, are you?"

Heddy's heart sank. Her plan was to grab a roll on her way out the door so she would have plenty of time in case Soli arrived early. Excuses about why she couldn't spend the day with Walter raced through her mind. Still, she had to be careful. Disgusting as the situation was, she had to show some interest in his advances.

"No, I don't work today. I'd love to have breakfast with you," she said with a smile. "I'm famished."

The two guards from her hallway followed them down the first flight of stairs.

"I hope you feel better today," Walter said.

For a quick second, Heddy considered why he was being mindful of her welfare then remembered she'd faked a headache the evening before. "Yes, thank you. A decent night's sleep is a good cure."

"Excellent." He stopped on his floor and put a finger in the air. "Ah, I forgot something in my room. Come with me."

What was he up to? He ordered his men to wait outside his door. Would it be safe for her?

Walter let her enter first and closed the door behind them.

"Sit," he said in a firm but polite voice. "I left some papers I need today."

He flipped through a pile of documents on a table. The container the professor had prepared for the Rembrandt painting was on the floor in the corner of the room. Walter caught her staring at it.

"Yes, Maus, that's the crate from the professor's office the other morning."

She played along and coyly tilted her head. "Yes, I noticed. It's a painting, isn't it?"

His eyes had an animated look while he explained. "Yes, a most exquisite work of art." He walked up to her and touched her chin. "But don't tell our Führer, all right? He doesn't need to know everything."

Heddy pressed forth a smile, trying to appear relaxed. "Of course not. What will you do with it?"

He straightened and returned to the pile of papers. "It's a surprise. One you may benefit from if all goes well."

"Intriguing. Will I like this painting?"

"No doubt you will. Although, I worry you might find the model more attractive than me." He threw his head back and laughed. "Good thing he's been dead for centuries."

"Will we hang it up in the house on Oscar Street?"

It was a daring question, but she needed something more steadfast—some piece of information she could give Soli later.

"Now, let's not talk more about that." He pulled a piece of paper from the middle of the pile. "Ah, there it is. Let's go have breakfast. I've planned a nice ride in the countryside today."

"Where to?" Heddy asked.

"You'll see."

They walked downstairs to the restaurant. What was she to do? The lieutenant colonel had the painting, but other than that, Heddy didn't have anything revolutionary to tell Soli.

A whiff of freshly baked goods and frying bacon met her at the door to the breakfast room. Heddy was indeed hungry. Staying at the hotel was costing more than she could afford already, and she'd skipped most of the meals there. But she was used to a sparse economy and little food. Walter led the way to a table by the window. The dining hall was half-full of guests, some she recognized from the party yesterday evening. They were German soldiers and local Nazi-supporters, some with their wives or mistresses. Heddy detested being there, but she pulled herself together and acted her part the best she could muster. One thing was certain: spying was not her favorite pastime.

"Put her meal on my bill," Walter said to the waitress who came to pour the coffee. He placed his jacket on the back of an empty chair and his visor cap on the table then winked at the girl.

With blushing cheeks, the poor thing nodded and slunk back to the kitchen.

At least one positive point about her morning—Heddy did not have to worry about how to pay for her meal.

The waitress returned with the trays. Fried eggs, several strips of bacon, slices of ham and cheese, and pieces of bread with butter and raspberry jam. A breakfast fit for royalty. For a moment, she'd simply enjoy the food and try not to feel guilty about her good fortune or for being there.

As usual, men came and went, visiting their table, speaking with Walter, and asking him about upcoming meetings and plans for the next days. There was music playing and the buzzing sound of people talking in the room. With her ears strained to the limit, Heddy picked up bits and pieces of the men's low conversations. She glanced out the window, pretending to be far away in thought. In fact, when Walter tried to get her attention, she ignored him the first time just to prove she hadn't listened in.

"Heddy...Heddy. What are you looking at?"

"Oh, I'm sorry. What did you say?"

He smiled but seemed a bit annoyed. "I asked what you were looking at."

"Oh, just the children playing with the dog on the

grass across the street. I think they are training it to sit on command."

"Well, they're enjoying themselves. As for me, I have work today and won't be able to take you for that ride, after all."

Her heart jumped for joy, but she tipped her head and gave him a half pout, half smile to indicate disappointment. She'd be fine on her own.

"I'm sorry, Maus. There's a meeting I must attend, but what are your plans today?"

Would she finally have some time to herself? Trying to conceal her excitement, she lowered her eyes and discreetly checked her wristwatch. Soli had probably waited an hour already. Oh, that her friend was patient just a little longer.

"I think I'll take a stroll down by the harbor, watch the waves in the sea, and listen to the seagulls...relax a bit," she said and smoothed her hair back.

"Such a romantic notion. I wish I could join you," he said and emptied his cup.

That's not my wish. Heddy gave him a pleasant smile, inwardly elated he wasn't joining her.

Walter stood and pushed in his chair. "My men will take you there."

"I don't need chaperones," Heddy said, her voice determined but friendly.

He pinched her cheek. "Silly you. Think of them as protectors."

"Do I need protecting? Who would harm me?"

"A woman as beautiful as you should be taken care of. My men will do that when I'm not present."

"But I tell you, it's not necessary."

He placed a finger on her lips then picked up his

uniform jacket and visor cap. "Hush, Maus. I know what's best for you, but I really must leave. Good day."

She sat for a moment after he'd left. *Mouse?* Why did a German man call his girlfriend a rodent? Growing up, she'd seen enough mice in her family's kitchen. The pests had eaten the food in their pantry and had ruined her favorite shoes. Gnawers were not something she associated with cuteness.

As inconspicuously as possible, Heddy grabbed the rest of the breakfast from the trays and folded it up into the napkin on her lap. She slipped the filled serviette into her purse. Soli would be happy about the bacon, ham, and fresh bread.

Walter's two guards stood in the corner talking as Heddy rose from her chair to leave. She didn't speak with them but walked outside. Were they following her? Hoping she'd gotten away by herself, she strode across the street in the direction of the harbor.

"Fräulein...wait, one moment, *bitte*...please."

Oh, no. They hadn't forgotten about her. The sturdy soldier marched next to her, his companion a few paces behind. Heddy swallowed hard. She'd like to speak her mind about robbing her privacy, but she couldn't.

"Does Fräulein want us to get the car?"

"No, thank you. It's not far. The harbor is only a couple of streets down that way."

Heddy kept walking, not encouraging any conversation. Certain Soli would understand the cryptic message, there was no exact hour for their rendezvous on the note. To meet at lunchtime was hopefully sufficient.

At the wharf, she parked herself on a bench overlooking the fiord. With the taste of salt on her lips and sprays of the ocean mist on her skin, she leaned back while her mind raced. What to do next? The two men sat on a stone barricade, their long legs dangling against the stone wall. Heddy had better hurry to the meeting point in hopes Soli hadn't left already.

She rose, walked up to the stone wall, and faced the men. "I need to go to the ladies' room. There's one in the small café over there. I'll be back soon."

The sturdy soldier nodded to her; his partner lit a cigarette.

Heddy had approached them first this time. Walter's men were always polite, never rude or misbehaving, but had she tried to run away, she'd probably see a different side to the guards. She started walking toward the seaside coffee shop, all the while straining her ears to hear if there were footsteps following her. On the pier in the distance, two men stood talking. *Arvid and Birger.* She'd recognize those two figures anywhere, and it gave her hope Soli was waiting inside. *Her team had arrived. She wasn't alone anymore.* She cast a quick glance over her shoulder as she entered the building. The soldiers were still sitting on the wall, smoking. No doubt they'd keep an eagle eye on the entrance to the café, knowing they'd be in trouble if they lost sight of her.

Heddy pushed the front door open and stepped across the threshold. Nikolai sat at one of the tables with a cup in his hands. Soli's handsome detective didn't look up at Heddy as she passed, but instead he stared toward the window while taking another sip. She continued through the room and to the restroom in the back. Her friends were prepared for her arrival, and Soli was waiting.

CHAPTER ELEVEN

NUME VALLEY, NORWAY, 1944

SOLI JUMPED FORWARD and wrapped her arms around Heddy as her friend entered the tiny lavatory in the back of the cafeteria.

"I finally managed to see you," Heddy said. "I want to explain what's going on, but I don't have much time. Walter's men are waiting outside."

Rolling her gaze around the restroom, Soli blurted out in a sarcastic tone, "A wonderful place to bump into friends. I remember well that day last year when we came in here and gobbled down blueberries until our teeth were blue."

"I was certain you'd understand where to meet me. We're used to speaking *Cryptian*, aren't we? As if that's even a language."

Soli smiled and glanced at her watch. "We have but a few minutes. Those men out there won't let you stay in here forever."

"Oh, Soli, it just feels good to be with my best friend after the last few days."

"So true. Now, tell me what happened that morning we were supposed to meet at Professor Holst's office to pick up Rembrandt's musketeer painting."

Heddy leaned her back against the wall. "I arrived early. The professor had prepared a sturdy crate for the painting. He wanted to show me how he'd placed the portrait inside and had just replaced the lid when Walter and his two baboons barged into the office." Heddy wrapped her arms around her stomach. "It all happened so fast. The men took the box with the painting, grabbed the professor, and then they came for me.

"I blurted out, 'I believe that old man has stolen a work of art. It belongs to the Reich. What should we do about it?'" Heddy closed her eyes for a moment and sighed. "Walter turned toward me, and his expression seemed intrigued by what I'd just said. I don't know what fell over me, Soli...it was the first thing I could think of to find out where they were taking the professor and the portrait."

Even though she was aware of her friend's never-faltering courage and sincere compassion with someone in need, Soli stood perplexed. Heddy had put herself in a situation so serious. Her gorgeous looks with those dark eyes and perfectly arched brows, the naturally rounded cheeks, and full bright-red lips no doubt enticed the German officer. How would she be able to escape his company now?

"What did Professor Holst say?" Soli asked. "I trust that man, but he could have said or done something to blow your cover."

"He struggled when the soldiers apprehended him but gave me a quick glance as if to acknowledge he under-stood what I was doing. It only took a second, but it was a feeling of mutual agreement about what we both needed to do. If the Gestapo had arrested me, as well, I wouldn't have been here to tell the story now. None of you would have known where to look for us."

"What happened to the professor? Do you know where they've taken him?"

Heddy shook her head. "Not yet, but I'm trying to fish for information."

Cramping knots in Soli's stomach forced her to squat. She lifted her gaze to Heddy's. "But think of the danger you put yourself in."

"I know, but you would have done the same to help that good, old archaeologist. I worry about the portrait, too. Your precious Rembrandt painting could have already been shipped out of the country."

Soli sighed. "Oh, I hope that's not true. So, what happened then?

"When Walter asked me if his driver could drop me off somewhere, I invented a story about working in the office next door for a few days and that I had just arrived on the morning train."

"How did you manage to find a vacant office?"

"Holst had mentioned something about an unoccupied room to me earlier. I took a chance, and later that day I broke in, using my hairpin. No one has claimed it yet. It just sits there empty."

"The maid who brought the note said you stayed at the Grand Hotel."

"Walter insisted on finding me a room there and bragged about their superior service. Of course, I can't afford it, but I'd started a dangerous game and couldn't back down. Not my best decision."

"How are we going to pay for it?"

"I don't know yet. I'm trying not to run the bill too high. Walter has paid for some of my meals, the rest I skip." She opened her purse and handed Soli the napkin with the food. "I almost forgot. This is from breakfast this morning."

Soli's mouth dropped open in surprise. "Oh, thank you. I'll share with the boys afterward." She placed the bundled-up serviette in her shoulder bag. "We'll find a way, Heddy. Try not to worry about the bill now." Soli tilted her head. "So, what is it you do at this office? Do you have a secret profession I haven't heard about?"

"Well, this is the most ridiculous part of this story. Walter asked me what I did all day." She pinched her face as if to swallow an oncoming giggle. "Sheep-farming."

Soli put both her hands in front of her lips to keep from laughing out loud. "What? Sheep-farming? Is that the best thing you could come up with? You could have simply said secretary or shop assistant."

"I know, but what's the fun in that? No, I'm being silly now. I guess it fell out of my mouth because sheep-farming is something I know a little about. I grew up spending the summers on my uncle's farm, herding sheep, and taking care of the new lambs. I loved it and learned a lot." She adjusted the belt on her coat. "Luckily, the lieutenant colonel has no interest in sheep farming. Once he heard about my boring research job, he never asked about it again."

"Fortunately, you didn't choose art as your work field."

"Oh, my goodness, no. I stayed clear of anything to do with art. But one thing is certain. Walter is extremely cautious. Those two soldiers follow me everywhere."

"Which means he doesn't really trust you."

"That man doesn't trust anyone. He yells at his men

and associates when he's dissatisfied. From what I've seen of him, he's a man who doesn't hide his thoughts or opinions. He's an open book and has a frightening temper. Sadly, I must play the obedient girlfriend. I'd hoped to be in and out of that hotel after one day, but when Walter makes up his mind, his determination seems unwavering."

"You mean since he likes you? I'm not surprised he does."

Heddy shivered. "Well, it's not a mutual liking. I've been part of many difficult operations during these last years, but this is by far the most uncomfortable. Just keeping that man at a distance is a chore. His reputation with women is certainly true. I picture Sverre in my mind while pretending to be interested."

"Do you think Walter knows who you are?"

"I hope not. At least, I don't think he knows I'm Heddy, the resistance advocate and leader of an underground organization—one who encourages and plans covert missions to thwart his plans. But Walter has probably made the connection to my late father, even though he has never mentioned it."

"Vengen is not a very common surname around here," Soli said.

"True, and I'm certain the position my father held in the Ministry of Communication—and his art interest, as well—brought the two together on more than one occasion. You know what a stout Nazi my father was."

Soli nodded. "He was the scary kind of wartime national socialist, totally engulfed in the principles of the Reich."

"Yes, he was, and even though the thought makes me sick to my stomach, I can only hope Walter thinks the same ideals run in my family. I never feel safe with the lieutenant colonel, but pretending to be on his side is my only protection right now."

Soli took Heddy's hands in hers. "But now we're here…together."

Heddy smiled and rolled her eyes around the small restroom. "It's Sunday, and the stores in town are closed. I would have much rather met you in the ladies' room at *Glassmagasinet*. Yesterday, at lunchtime, I left the office, making up errands."

"I noticed the skirt. You didn't have any clothes or toiletries when you ran off, did you?"

Heddy laughed low. "No, nothing. Since I couldn't have those two guards follow me to your art store, I pretended to go shopping on my lunch break. A cousin of mine has a small shop, and she let me borrow some clothes for a few days. I needed a couple of nice outfits and a dinner dress."

"I'm glad. She took a great risk doing such a thing."

"Yes, she did. I trust her not to tell anyone."

"That's good." Soli shrugged weakly. "We've all been so worried about you."

"I know, and I'm sorry. My meanderings through the streets always led me to the square by Our Savior's Church, hoping to see you, Nikolai, or the boys across the street. I thought I saw Birger and Arvid on their way through the iron gate to the crypt one day, and I wanted to call out or run to the corner to see them. But I held back. It would have ruined my mission, and I couldn't compromise the situation I've put myself in."

"That could very well have been them. Those two are loyal and dedicated. They've searched for you ever since the first moment they didn't hear from you."

"I'm sorry to upset them, but I don't see how I could have done it differently. I made the decision fast and didn't have the time to think through the details. I didn't want to worry all of you, but I understand that's exactly what I did."

"You must feel lonely."

"Oh, I did. But not so much anymore now I've been able to talk with you and hear our boys are safe, but I keep thinking about the professor. We must find him, and I pray he's still alive."

There was a knock on the door. A woman's voice outside the restroom said, "Are you done soon?"

"One moment please." Soli leaned in and whispered to Heddy, "We'll find the professor. Before you go, tell me what you know about the painting?"

Heddy answered low. "Walter's hotel room is well-guarded, and he always has someone outside the door. But this morning he invited me in, and I saw the crate on the floor." She frowned. "I still don't know who told him about the portrait, and I have no clue what Walter's plans are."

"Well, we'll keep on searching." Soli glanced at her watch again. "I don't want you to leave, but I think it's best. That woman outside the door is waiting, and we don't want Walter's guards to barge in here looking for you."

Heddy picked up her purse. "I'll tell them I had stomach problems. They won't ask me to elaborate. For now, I'll act my part until I can find out where the professor and the painting are." She closed her eyes. "Every night when I'm alone in my room, I throw up. That's how repulsive this situation is."

Soli hugged her fiercely. "I wish we didn't have to part, but it's time. Be careful."

"I will." Heddy pulled her shoulders back and opened the door. With her head held high, she passed the waiting woman and walked outside.

With the door still open, Soli pretended to wipe her hands on the towel next to the tiny sink. She smiled at the woman. "I apologize for the delay."

She joined Nikolai who was keeping watch at the table close to the window.

CHAPTER TWELVE

A FEW HOURS later, Soli entered Oscar Street carrying a small suitcase. A chilly breeze swept across the residential area. At one point, she had to hold on to her cloche hat to keep it from blowing away. She fastened the top button on her coat. No wonder the lane seemed quiet. Citizens and soldiers were most likely indoors, either holding a cup of something warm to drink or resting up before a new week of hard work.

Soli had arranged to meet Nikolai and the boys at Ruber's mansion. They'd decided to arrive separately. After they'd gathered the remaining artwork hidden in the house, they'd leave the same way, each carrying part of the collection. A full operation with all of them together and driving Arvid's old truck would be too obvious. Nikolai had no available car at the police station, either. Walking the few streets back to her art shop seemed like the best choice, but she wouldn't be all by herself. At the first sign of trouble, Nikolai and the boys would be close behind her.

Such a tedious task, planning every detail of her days to avoid danger. At times, she dreamed of strolling downtown Oslo—hand in hand with Nikolai—sitting on a bench overlooking the fiord, eating ice cream, and resting her head on his shoulder without checking the area for soldiers, Nazis, or Heinz Walter.

Oh, what a horrible man that lieutenant colonel was, causing distress wherever he went. Now, because of Heddy's compromising act to befriend him, Walter had become much too close for comfort. Soli couldn't blame her friend for her impromptu choice. Wouldn't she have done the same, had she been in Heddy's situation? Even though it seemed like the cleverest solution to find the information they needed, Heddy had put her life in continuous danger. Soli detested how Walter kept her friend under surveillance. At least, tonight, they'd remove the rest of the Ruber family's artwork and keep it away from that German officer's greedy hands. Then their next mission would be to find the professor and the musketeer painting. Time was not on their side. Walter could be shipping the Rembrandt off today, tomorrow, or the following day. He could seriously hurt the professor and may have even already shot him.

As Soli approached the iron gate, she noticed Nikolai by the entrance to the mansion. He was probably picking the lock. Two seconds later, he pushed the door open and entered. Soli walked up the path and slipped inside, closing the door behind her.

As she placed the suitcase on the floor, Nikolai grabbed her and planted a soft kiss on her lips. "Hello, lovely lady. Welcome to my humble abode."

"Silly you, Nikolai. Concentrate on why we're here."

"Oh, I am. I'm concentrating on you and me...here."

She melted at the expression in his dark-blue eyes and leaned her head against his chest, reminding herself of wonderful things in her life, such as her feelings for Nikolai and having him return that love.

Someone grabbed the door handle, and Nikolai quickly let go of Soli, pulled her behind his back, and held a hand on the gun in his inside coat pocket. In that moment, she panicked. Had Walter come to look at the manor again? Was Heddy with him? Or was someone else there to pick up any remaining items?

When Birger's cheerful face poked through the open door, Soli took a step back and breathed.

Arvid followed. "You look like you've seen a ghost?" He shut the door and flipped the lock.

"I don't know...I just..." Soli started laughing. "I was in such a serious disposition on my way over here, making plans for what we needed to accomplish in the next few days and trying to encourage myself. I tell you, giving yourself a pep talk can be exhausting, and then Nikolai—"

Birger grinned. "We get it. The detective changed the mood completely."

Soli smiled. "Yes, he did." She straightened her back. "But now to work. All the major art pieces that hung on the wall were sold at auctions or confiscated by the Gestapo. We found one painting hidden in the chimney earlier, so that one has been taken to safety. We don't have much time, but Arvid and Birger, could you two go through every room in the house and see if you find any other hiding places? Think about Mr. Ruber and how fond he was of riddles. He came up with ingenious ways to hide artwork from the Nazis."

Arvid nodded. "We're on it. Come, Birger. Let's start upstairs."

Nikolai peeked through the door to the former dining area and then into the living room. He turned to Soli. "We need to hurry. Put me to work. Where should I look?"

"You, sir, will have the honor of opening the doors to where Isaac Ruber hid another part of his art collection. When I was here with Heddy and Rolf a while back, we were initially looking for the seventeenth century portrait of Annarosa."

"The Ruber family's foremother?"

Soli nodded. "Yes, but as we followed clues written in the old ledger, we stumbled upon an extraordinary assortment of unmounted prints. At the time, we couldn't take everything, but now, Nikolai...if you would do the honors."

He raised his eyebrows. "And do what?"

She flipped her hand. "This way." She went to stand at the bottom of the staircase. "See those decorative wings carved into the siding next to the three first steps?"

Nikolai kneeled to take a closer look. "Why wings?"

"They represent Mercury, the god of merchants. Isaac Ruber used the symbol as a clue to his wealth. He hid something very valuable inside there."

Nikolai raised his shoulders. "Where?"

She put the palm of her hand flat against the first step's nosing. "Press here."

He leaned in and pushed his hand against the wood, and the riser opened like a drawer. Nikolai gawked. "How did you know?"

"I told you. I just followed the leads Isaac Ruber recorded in his journal. He had quite an imagination."

"It's brilliant," Nikolai said and opened the drawer all the way.

A pile of etchings and drawings stared back at them.

Soli's heart leaped. Her lifelong passion for art burst forth, and it was as if her whole body smiled with happiness.

Nikolai took hold of her hand and pulled her down on the floor next to him. "Come here, you. Sit with me. These moments when you are overwhelmed with joy and enthusiasm about finding art to preserve and keep safe are precious. I love you for it...I love you."

Stunned, she looked at his handsome face. He'd never said those words out loud to her before. Nikolai was gallant and protective, forever her kind and chivalrous detective, but he was not always a man who professed his feelings with words.

She smoothed her cheek against his and whispered in his ear, "I love you, too."

They sat for a moment, separate from the dangers of their operation, savoring their twinkling of joy in an unstable world.

"We should finish," Nikolai finally said, his voice soft.

She nodded and turned her attention to the artwork in the drawer. "There are two more drawers like this one—both full of beautiful pieces." She picked up a couple of etchings. "Here's one by our own Edvard Munch, and these two are by Francisco de Goya and Antoine Watteau. There are several by Jean Baptiste Corot. Look at all these."

Arvid and Birger descended the stairs and sat down on the steps above the open drawer.

"We didn't find anything else," Arvid said.

Birger grinned. "But that's quite a treasure, Soli. Are we bringing all of them? There must be a hundred engravings."

"We'll take the whole collection," Nikolai said. "Walter won't get his greedy fingers on a single one of these. I suggest we hide them in Soli's basement. There's no time to take them out of town, as we need all hands on deck to help Heddy."

"That's probably best, Nikolai," Soli said. "Since the National Art Gallery is not functioning now, and I don't trust other curators, we should just hide these in my secret room for now. But I warn you, I'll be up all night studying these."

"I don't doubt it," Nikolai said and winked at her. "But first, we need to get them safely through the streets of Oslo."

"We can do it. We'll each carry some and keep an eye on one another from a distance." Arvid nodded toward the front entrance. "Birger and I put our shoulder bags on the floor by the door."

"Mine is there, too," said Nikolai.

"I'll get them." Soli hurried to the door and returned with the bags and her suitcase. She handed them out. "Now, please be careful as you handle the prints. Don't fold any corners or bend them in any way."

Swiftly, but with caution, they filled their bags then closed the three empty drawers.

Nikolai walked to the door. "Birger, you go first, then Soli. Keep your distance. Arvid and I will form the rear troop. Now, hurry. I'll lock up here. See you all at the art shop in about half an hour."

MONDAY, 30 APRIL 1945

CHAPTER THIRTEEN

HEDDY STOOD IN FRONT of the mirror in her hotel room, putting the finishing touches to her lipstick. What would this new week bring? She walked out into the hallway and hurried toward the staircase. Her goal was to eat an early breakfast before Walter showed up at the table. His two men lounged at the end of the corridor, talking. They sauntered after her, pretending to leave her alone, but both she and they knew that was not the case.

Only a few of the tables in the dining area were occupied. What if she crossed the room and headed for the exit? Tempted by the idea, she scanned the area. If she left now, she might avoid meeting the lieutenant colonel altogether. As she approached the door to the street, the man himself entered. *Think of the devil, and he will appear...* She quickly found a seat at a table close to the door, picked up the menu, and didn't look his way until he stood next to her.

"Good morning, beautiful." He sat down and snapped his fingers at the waitress.

The young maid rushed to his side and curtsied.

"We'll have our normal breakfast," he said and leaned back in the chair.

"Yes, sir." The girl scurried to the kitchen.

"Now, Heddy. I have a full day, but I'd like you to accompany me to the Ruber residence later today. Have you given any thought to the interior there? I need a woman's touch when I plan the redecorating. It's a fine mansion, and I can't wait to spend time with you there alone, away from both of our busy schedules."

An older German officer approached them and began talking low with Walter. Both men were clearly agitated by news about German troops in Italy. From what Heddy could make out, the German command in that country had signed a surrender the day before. Walter hit his fist on the table. His expression was hard and brutal, as if he had a difficult time controlling his anger. Heddy stayed quiet, and when the waitress placed a plate in front of her, Heddy started eating right away without waiting for Walter.

The men kept up their quiet discussion. Heddy swallowed her last bite and pushed her chair back.

"Excuse me, but I need to get ready for work. We'll speak later."

Walter nodded to her then continued his conversation with the older officer. The two guards stood outside the main door, smoking. Heddy hurried up the stairs, and as she reached the first landing, she paused and turned around. The guards were not behind her. Walter's room was the first on the right, and the door was wide open. This might be her best chance yet. Heddy peeked inside. The maid who had helped her before was making the bed. The girl hummed as she smoothed the sheet and fluffed the eiderdown quilt and pillow. She turned her head and smiled as Heddy entered.

Heddy closed the door, leaving it slightly ajar, and put a finger to her lips. "I just need to pick up something," she said and proceeded to the crate on the floor.

The girl nodded and continued her work.

If Heddy could get to the back staircase at the other end of the hallway before the guards appeared, she could be out on the street in no time and run through a passageway on the other side. In the alley, she could easily move into an adjacent garden and exit on a different road. Her cousin's shop was in that vicinity, and Heddy planned to leave the crate with the painting there until she had a safe route to carry it to Soli's shop or the crypt. If she could pull this off, the last days would have been worth it. Then finding the professor would be her next priority. Since she'd heard no mention of Holst so far, it might be better to find a new approach to learn where they'd taken him…if the old man was still alive.

The crate was large and a bit awkward to carry. Heddy gripped the outside edges and carried it vertically in front of her chest. The maid kept dusting the furniture and deliberately seemed to avoid noticing Heddy walking away with the wooden box in her arms. Suddenly, the door burst open, and there stood Walter.

"What is going on here?" he thundered. He grabbed the maid's arm. "Leave us."

The girl curtsied and pushed the cleaning cart out of the room.

Quickly, Heddy. Think of something clever to say.

"I was curious about the beautiful painting you mentioned yesterday morning. So, when I was on my way out, I saw your door open and thought you wouldn't mind if I had a look. After all, you wanted me to come up with ideas for the house on Oscar Street."

Walter's eyes darted fire. "Your room is not on this floor, Heddy, and you're holding the crate. Were you actually going to open it without my permission? That painting is mine. No one touches it."

The Rembrandt painting of the musketeer was definitely not his. The lieutenant colonel had stolen it from the professor, who'd found the portrait next to a corpse, who happened to be a thief who had in turn stolen it from a member of the Ruber family centuries ago. Ergo, in no way did it belong to Walter. He was only a powerful man filled with greed and selfish motives.

Heddy's insides were utter chaos. *Calm down. Act your part and do something sensible.* She placed the crate on the bed. "I was only going to put it here and have a peek. I thought you'd be pleased that I was proactive in helping you consider what would be appropriate for the manor."

His men were right behind him, blocking any hope of escape. Heddy walked up to Walter, stroked her hand on his arm, and offered a sweet smile.

He pushed her hand away. "Who are you really?"

"I'm Heddy Vengen; you know me."

"Obviously, I don't. I have no idea who you are." He started pacing the floor. "Although, I've only met your father on a few occasions, I learned Carl Vengen was a true supporter of the Reich. He was also interested in art, as am I. What happened to him? I haven't seen him for a while."

"He passed away."

"Ah, I should offer my condolences, but at this point, I have no sympathy for you whatsoever. You entered my private quarters—uninvited—and I caught you on your way out with my painting."

"But I—"

"Oh, spare me your tears and explanations, Heddy." Walter spun to his men. "This is a snag in my plans. Our cute *Maus* has turned into a red-lipped rat. I need to change my agenda."

"What should we do with her?" one of the men asked.

"I'm not sure yet. I need to think. Just get rid of her. But not here. Somewhere remote."

The other guard took a step forward. "How about that place...you know?"

Walter nodded.

"Jawohl, Herr Kommandant," the soldier answered and seized Heddy's arm.

"Let me go or I'll scream," she hissed.

"Ha! You could try. Not much good it would do you." Walter walked to the window. "Take her away then come back for me. I have plans for the painting."

Heddy gazed over her shoulder as the two men dragged her out of the room. The lovely musketeer portrait was left there with that egocentric, ruthless villain. She'd been in desperate situations many times before, but at this moment, she could not see a happy ending. She kicked and struggled with all her strength until one of the men pulled out his gun and pressed it against her back. The other one tied her hands and dragged her down the back stairs and into a car. The door slammed shut, and the engine started. People walked by on the sidewalk on the other side of the street, and there was a man nonchalantly leaning against the wall, reading a newspaper. The guy wore a herringbone cap, knicker-bockers, and a taupe, double-breasted jacket. A sense of recognition hit her. Perplexed, she watched him through the car window as they drove away. The man folded up his newspaper and disappeared around the corner.

Then, abruptly, the soldier in the passenger seat pulled a black hood over her head. She struggled to get the sack off, but with her hands tied behind her back she had no luck.

"Sit still," one of the soldiers commanded.

No more politeness or addressing her as *Fräulein*. They'd caught her in the act of taking the painting, and now, she was nothing more than a minor problem to get rid of.

Heddy leaned back, closing her eyes. That man on the sidewalk... Was he Sverre? No, her beloved was in Sweden. She longed for him to come rescue her and take her away from this mess she'd put herself in. Wishful thinking? Perhaps...but it had certainly looked like him.

She concentrated on where they could be driving. Straight ahead, along a circular street, then a right bend. They were headed eastward out of town. Seagulls cried by the fiord, and the smell of saltwater penetrated the car. The dull sound of going through a short tunnel. Then she lost her direction. *Where on Earth are they taking me?*

The car changed course once again. Gone were the sounds of traffic and people. The road seemed curvy with hills and bends. After a sharp turn to the right, the car advanced up a gravel road. As the terrain leveled, the driver parked and turned off the engine. Someone opened her door and dragged her out. They steered her up a narrow path then down three solid steps. A key turned in a lock, hinges squeaked, and she was pushed across a threshold and into a room.

Heddy stood completely still. Where was she?

The crunch of the lock and the car driving back down the gravel road told her the soldiers had left her alone. She had to get out of there. Wriggling her wrist didn't help. The rope wouldn't budge. Slowly, she moved her feet backward, hoping to find the door's hinges or handle. If she rubbed the cord against the metal, she might be able to tear the twine and remove the sack from her head.

"Heddy?"

She froze. The voice sounded tired and hoarse but familiar. Someone took hold of her. When she tried to move away, that person grabbed the sack and pulled it off. At first, she must have looked both frightened and aggressive, but as she gazed into the old man's eyes, her shoulders relaxed.

"It's me, Heddy. Professor Holst. Let me get those ropes off your wrists."

He untied the cord, and Heddy flung her arms around his neck.

"There, there, my dear," the professor said and patted her back. "You're all right now."

They were in a small basement. White-washed brick walls with a narrow window, a round table, and a couple of chairs. When Heddy saw the pitiful state of what food they'd left for Holst—a few bottles of water and stale bread—she wished she'd wrapped up some of her scrumptious breakfast from the Grand Hotel. She'd had more than enough on her plate to share. There was also a bucket in the corner, some newspapers, and a woolen blanket on the concrete floor. A steep, ladder-type staircase was in the back of the room. Holst noticed her staring at it. "That goes to the cabin upstairs. I've tried to kick in the door at the top, but it wouldn't budge. You're welcome to try."

"What about where I entered?" Heddy asked. "It goes out, doesn't it?"

She started toward the door and was about to grab the handle when the professor yelled.

"Stop! The lock is wired. They warned me about some sort of explosive contraption on the outside."

Heddy put a hand on her chest. "Oh, my goodness. I'm glad you told me in time." She headed toward the stairs. "I'll just check the other exit—unless you think that's wired, as well."

"No, it's not. I've heard the men talking. I believe only the main entrance and this basement door have explosives attached."

Heddy hurried up the rickety staircase and tried to pick the lock with a bobby pin from her hair. "I can unlock it," she said, "but something else seems to be preventing the door from opening. It wiggles a little, but I can't seem to push it forward. Perhaps there's a padlock on the other side."

"Yes, that could be it." The professor sat down on one of the chairs. "Come back down here and tell me what happened to you."

Heddy took a seat and explained the last few days since they were so roughly parted. "I'm so sorry for leaving you, but it was the only way I could think of to discover where those beasts were taking you and the painting."

He looked at her with understanding. "And now you've found me."

"Well, I can't take credit for finding you. I was forced here."

Bruises covered Holst's kindly face. Redness in his

droopy eyes had replaced the enthusiastic glow they'd held when Heddy had first met him.

"Oh, what have they done to you, Professor? I wish they'd taken me instead of you."

"I'm fine, Heddy. Thank goodness, I had nothing much to tell them. I've a feeling they might have tried to squeeze more information out of you had they only known where to start. That German lieutenant colonel is only a narcissistic treasure hunter. I've met one or two like him during my career. Fortunately, he only knows bits and pieces about where to look for hidden art."

"Who told him about the Rembrandt?"

"Jesper, one of the two assistants at the dig. A Danish fellow. This was his first job with me. I'd interviewed him and had thoroughly checked his qualifications. As I said earlier...I trusted him."

"That explains why Walter knew exactly where to find the painting."

The professor nodded. "I should have been more careful, but the man came highly recommended by one of my Danish colleagues."

"Still, anyone can be tempted once they have a treasure within their grasp. Jesper probably thought he could earn a good reward for revealing the information to Walter."

"Exactly." The professor leaned forward, his elbows on his thighs. "Well, what's done is done."

Heddy was not about to give up. She would do everything she could to get the professor out of the cabin and then find out where the lieutenant colonel was taking the painting. With the rumors of Hitler's imminent surrender, Walter seemed more tense than ever. Stressed people made mistakes. The pursuit of finding the musketeer portrait was far from over. She was not about to lie down and starve to death in the musty basement of a remote cottage.

She pushed her chair closer to the professor's. "Most folks have their own agenda these days. Even me. There I was at the Grand Hotel, a resistance woman to the core, pretending to enjoy being courted by a German officer. I was sick to my stomach and wanted to run away, get out of his clutches, but I'd set myself in a difficult position and had started something without telling my group about my personal *Operation Heinz Walter*. Finding you and the painting was foremost in my mind."

"And I thank you for that," the professor said low, his eyes expressing sympathy. "You look tired, Heddy. Maybe you should rest."

Heddy appreciated the professor's concern, but she couldn't relax now. She'd slept little at the Grand Hotel. Most nights, she'd stared into space, wondering how she could keep up the pretense with a man like Walter. Hopefully, Sverre would forgive her. Soli's brother meant everything to Heddy.

~ CAPITOLO IV ~

AMSTERDAM, HOLLAND
MID-AUGUST 1641

CLAUDE SADDLED HIS horse and urged the stallion into a canter until he reached the roadhouse. He barged through the front door. Candles lit up each table in the dim room. He'd been there before. The tavern was popular and attracted all sorts of townspeople. Claude nodded to the innkeeper behind the counter as he stepped into the center of the room. A dog crossed the floor in front of him, and a group of young men were benched down on both sides of a long table playing a game with dice, cards, and wooden sticks. A woman walked around, pouring ale into empty jugs. In the back corner, Claude spotted the two men who'd stood waiting with an extra horse outside his gate. They sat facing each other in a booth, both holding ale mugs. Where was the other culprit, the one Claude and Annarosa had fought in the garden?

Claude marched up to their table, firmly planted his feet in a broad stance, and gave the two a disapproving stare. They jumped, wide-eyed, from their seats, but before they could draw a knife or weapon, he grabbed both scoundrels in a solid hold, twisting their arms in a position clearly uncomfortable and painful to the men.

"Let go," the man with a scar down his left cheek hissed.

Claude pushed both down into their seats and pulled out his sword and held it close to the scarred man's face. "I want to speak with you both about an incident earlier tonight. And if you behave...you, my good fellow, won't get a matching mark on your other cheek."

The scarred man gave several quick, tense nods.

Still pointing his sword toward the men, Claude scanned the room. The culprit was nowhere in sight, and the rest of the guests kept to themselves, pretending they didn't see what was going on.

Claude called out to the innkeeper by the counter. "Send someone to fetch the militia guard." He then turned back to the men at the table. "Now, where's your friend, the one with raven-colored hair...the one who wears a floppy blue hat?"

When they didn't answer right away, Claude tightened the grip on his sword and lowered his chin, giving them a strict stare through his eyelashes.

The man with the scarred cheek urged his freckled friend across the table. "You tell him."

The other fellow swallowed nervously. These two were clearly not in charge of the heist but merely hired to do the ringleader's bidding. And where was that scoundrel now? Had he disappeared with the painting? Had he even paid these fellows anything to assist him?

The freckled man cleared his throat. "Wolfert said he'd give us compensation once the painting was sold. He's leaving on a ship tonight. Said the buyer was someone influential."

"Wolfert, huh? And where exactly will this ship take your friend?"

The freckled man stared in disbelief. "He's not our friend. We just arranged for the horses."

Two uniformed men from the militia guard entered the tavern. Following the innkeeper's instruction, the guards strode toward their table. Claude explained the situation and asked them not to go too hard on the thieves. He was more interested in finding Wolfert and retrieving the Rembrandt portrait, knowing Annarosa's heart would break if they lost it forever.

On his way out, he handed the innkeeper a coin. With a quick nod, Claude exited the tavern and mounted his horse. The harbor was not far.

* * *

Wolfert sat on the ship's deck, attaching a braided rope to the wooden tube with the rolled-up painting. He'd made it—safe from the militia guard, safe from the wrath of the Frenchman and his wife, safe from Dutch artists who'd probably form an armed band and hunt him down if they grasped what he was doing.

The heist had been planned down to the smallest detail. Wolfert had been rubbing his hands ever since he'd heard the Frenchman and his wife had four valuable paintings. Unfortunately, the couple had arrived home too soon and had ruined Wolfert's chance of stealing the lot. Imagine how much he could have sold a four-leaf-clover like that for. Well, the rest of the collection was still there for the taking. He sighed. Next time.

And what about the two gullible clowns he'd hired for the getaway? They'd stood outside the gate with the horses, holding the first painting as he went back for more. Trustworthy and on time, they were. A rarity these days. Wolfert had to admit he'd been quite nervous as he'd run away from the Frenchman and had barely escaped. But he had, and from there he'd taken the artwork directly to the beekeeper woman by the park. She'd acceded to his request and had prepared a most excellent wooden tube and warm wax. Working with precision and speed, the woman had removed the frame and sealed the container with the portrait inside.

On his instruction, the beekeeper woman had pressed his seal with the letter W—an extravagant addition he flaunted on everything he sold—into the drying wax. Using such a seal gave him the air of a merchant instead of a lowly thief. Pleased with the result, he left her the elaborately carved, gilded frame as payment. She could either use it herself or sell it for a good price at the town market.

He'd never stolen an original Rembrandt before, only a couple of sketches by the master painter's students. Not that most buyers would know the difference, and he hadn't heard any complaints so far. The whole idea was exhilarating and his success encouraging.

Yes, except for the sudden return of the French musketeer and his sword-wielding wife, this robbery had gone well and according to Wolfert's plan. He ran his finger along the thick layer of dried beeswax that sealed the top of the wooden tube. It was perfect and could withstand any weather, although he hoped Mother Nature would be good to him on the trip. He already shivered from the cool wind across the ocean, and the flesh-wound across his lower chest was acting up. Hopefully, it would not become infected. Wretched woman. Wolfert honestly had not expected her to slash the tip of her sword through his coat. Yes, she was carrying a deadly weapon, but the beauty was a feminine work of art. What a disguise. Where on Earth had she learned to handle her sword and move like that?

He finished the last knot on the thin rope and fastened it to the wooden tube. With the braided string around his neck, he rested the tube in his lap. The ship swayed with the waves. The movement did not bother him. He'd spent enough time at sea, going to distant shores to fight in more battles than he wished to remember.

Wolfert pulled a satisfied grin. That old maid was quite a character. Had it not been for the seriousness of the robbery, he would have laughed out loud when she'd kicked his shin and had even bit him as he'd shoved the cloth into her mouth. Tying her hands had not been too difficult before he'd locked her up. In honesty, he admired elderly women who fought for themselves. He'd once had a mother like that.

Now, off to see the buyer. The collector up north would pay a considerable sum of *kroner* for the Rembrandt musketeer portrait. The man usually paid well for a fine piece of artwork.

Wolfert pulled his hat farther down until the droopy brim covered half his face. They still had hours at sea before they reached the Norwegian shores, and he didn't trust the passengers who wandered the deck, looking like they had dubious intentions. Clutching the container closer, Wolfert stayed wide awake, keeping his guard up.

CHAPTER FOURTEEN

SORKEDALEN, NORWAY 30 APRIL 1945

HEDDY CHECKED HER wristwatch...again. She'd tried everything. The basement window was too narrow to climb through, but she was glad to have the natural light streaming into the room. It also gave them a connection to the outside world. Unfortunately, both doors seemed impenetrable, and there was no one around to help them. Finally, she sank down on the floor, her head in her hands, and let the tears run freely.

"Come now, dear." The professor stroked her hair. "I haven't lived to be an old man and survive years of wretched war, only to die in a basement in Sorkedalen."

Heddy looked up. "Sorkedalen? You know where we are?" She hadn't even thought to ask him—maybe because it didn't matter—but she was acquainted with this valley, the surrounding woodland, and the roads. The knowledge gave her confidence and hope that if they could only escape, she knew how to get them back to Oslo.

The sound of an approaching car on the gravel road startled her. "Professor, they're here again." She stood, wiped her cheeks with the back of her hand, and ran to the narrow window. "I can't see the car from here. We must be on the back side of the cabin."

Holst nodded. "Why don't you go sit at the top of the stairs and see if you can pick up any conversation through the door? Your hearing is much better than mine."

Heddy crept up the stairs, careful not to make a sound on the creaking steps. She sat down at the top with her ear against the door. She strained to form a picture of what was happening on the other side. Hinges creaked and several heavy boots stomped into the cabin. What if they'd come to interrogate her and the professor? If they did, she'd hear them coming and hurry down the staircase.

"Can you pick up what they're saying?" Holst whispered.

Heddy put three fingers in the air and mouthed, "Three men."

She closed her eyes to concentrate on the conversation. She identified Walter's firm German accent. She didn't know the names of the two men who'd kept her under surveillance the last few days, but it was them...the first, a thin soldier with a high-pitched voice and the second, a sturdy fellow who spoke with a hoarse, calm intonation.

"Careful. I need that musketeer painting in top shape," Walter said in a commanding tone.

"Where do you want it?" the first man asked.

"In the attic with the other art pieces, and make sure they're well hidden. Even with the extra protection on the doors, someone might be able to break in here."

"*Jawohl, Herr Obersturmbannführer.*"

There were various sounds on the other side of the door. Heddy guessed the thin soldier opened an attic hatch using a rod with a hook at the end, released the pull-down ladder, and climbed up with the crate. A few minutes later, it sounded as if he'd returned.

Walter spoke again. "It's getting late. Take me back to the hotel. Tomorrow, we drive to my appointment with Haraldsen."

"The pastor?" the soldier with the hoarse voice asked.

"I suppose he was a pastor once," Walter said. "But there's not much religion in that man anymore. I'd say he's more of an eccentric recluse living in a parsonage. Although, I'd call him an art connoisseur most definitely. He's especially interested in art by Flemish masters. And there's nothing better than a Rembrandt then, is there? I'll negotiate a good price for the painting and should be able to squeeze a considerable sum out of him. When that's done, you two will return here, pick up the portrait, and bring it to me."

"And what about those two downstairs?"

"Leave them there for now. We don't have time to deal with them at the moment. My priority is the meeting with Mr. Haraldsen." Walter paused then said, "It's a shame, really. That woman may be gorgeous, but she's not to be trusted."

"Do you want us to get rid of them?" the soldier with the high-pitched voice asked.

"Let me think about it until you return for the painting. Most likely, we don't need her or the professor anymore." Walter made a short pause again. "And that art historian...the one who's taken over Holm's art shop?" He snapped his fingers twice. "What was her name? Soli Hansen? Yes, that's it. Keep her under surveillance. I can't trust anyone right now."

The door slammed shut, and the cabin was once again

deserted. Heddy sank back on the stairs and slumped against the wall as the car drove away. What if Walter found out about Soli's involvement with the resistance?

"They left the Rembrandt here," she said as she despondently slunk down the stairs. "It's in the attic."

"Why the sad face? That's a good thing, Heddy. We just need to get into the rooms upstairs."

"I know." She wiped her clammy hands on her skirt and pushed her hair behind her ears. The professor didn't need another worry. Walter had asked his men to keep a close watch on Soli. Didn't they have other things to do? She took a breath and presented a thin smile. "Is there anything else down there we can use to break open the door at the top of the stairs?"

The professor circled the floor, his feet dragging. "Let's scour the room. Perhaps we'll find something I've overlooked."

They combed the room, searching every corner. Next to the waste bucket, under a pile of old newspapers, the professor found a hammer with a wooden handle and a box of nails.

"I can't believe I missed this when I looked before," Holst said and handed Heddy the mallet.

"I can absolutely use it." She hurried back up and started banging on the door.

"Don't fall down the stairs," Holst said. "Be careful."

"I'm all right. The door is moving now. Just a bit more. I see a chain with a padlock through the crack."

Heddy pounded with all the strength she could muster, but it was not enough to break the chain. She felt as if she'd hammered for hours. The professor came up behind her, and they took turns using the hammer while the light of day slowly withdrew from the basement.

"Heddy, dear, please come down. Get some rest now. Let's continue tomorrow."

"Just a little more. Those men could show up here again at any moment."

"It'll be dark soon. The lightbulb in the ceiling is broken, and we have no candles or matches."

Heddy descended the stairs. Outside the narrow window, the foreboding sky had turned a charcoal gray.

"There's no moon tonight, either." She let out a frustrated breath. "Everything is against us."

"Try to be positive. We'll continue as soon as the first rays of light stream through that windowpane."

Heddy sighed at the sight of her blistered right hand. "My friend Soli is usually the positive one. She thinks differently from me and finds solutions when I bang my head against the wall."

"Ah, yes, she's creative, even in the way she handles practical challenges. I remember that from when she was a student. She was not like the others." The professor poured some water in the cup on the table and handed it to Heddy.

She shook her head. "Oh, no, you drink that. There's not much left."

"No, Heddy, I had some earlier. You've been working on that door for hours, and you'll be no use to either of us if you pass out. We'll share what we have, and that's it."

Heddy offered a thin smile. Although weak and tired, the old man was determined. She accepted the cup, drank half of the water, then handed it back.

The professor finished the rest then spread the newspapers on the cold floor. He sat down and patted the space next to him. "Come, lie down here and get some sleep.

Heddy did as she was told and placed her head in his

lap while he covered her with the woolen blanket. Holst then leaned back against the brick wall.

He was like the grandfather she'd never had—kind, generous, and wise. Soon, he was sleeping soundly. Wound up by the day's events, Heddy stared into the darkness. Not that she planned on staying in this uninhabited cabin, but she'd carved a notch on the wooden frame around the door with the hammer. The idea came from a book Soli had told Heddy about, called *The Count of Monte Cristo*. In Alexandre Dumas's novel, a young man was falsely imprisoned and carved lines for all the days and then years he spent locked up. Heaven forbid they'd have to stay there long. How many days would she and the professor survive? Food was scarce. The dry bread was mostly gone now. Would Walter and his men come back with more water and supplies, or would they be true to their word and simply get rid of the professor and her?

What would tomorrow bring? Soli would be opening her art shop in a few hours, worried out of her mind because she hadn't heard anything more from Heddy. The boys would probably keep close watch on the hotel, and Nikolai would no doubt try to obtain information about Walter's agenda. They'd most likely involved Rolf, had probably asked him for advice. And Sverre? He was in Stockholm. If he knew she was in trouble, he'd come across the border and do everything in his power to find her...to rescue her. Oh, how she missed him. He'd filled her heart from the first moment she'd met him, and even though they'd spent much time apart, he was still the love of her life.

Closing her eyes, she drifted off to sleep, feeling unreservedly disheartened.

CHAPTER FIFTEEN

OSLO, NORWAY

SOLI CLIMBED THE LAST flight of stairs to Rolf's apartment on the east side of Oslo. She brushed the rain off her shoulders and removed her cloche hat as she knocked on the door.

Nikolai opened and kissed her cheek. "They're all here. Did you check that no one followed you?"

"Yes, I was very careful."

Nikolai looked out toward the stairwell then closed the door behind them. Soli hung her coat on a hanger in the wardrobe and placed her shoes on the floor. Birger and Arvid stood by the window in the living room and nodded to her as she entered.

Rolf sat on the couch, looking frailer than the last time Soli had seen him.

He moved his cane out of the way and stretched out his arms. "Give me a hug, Soli. I need some sunshine right now."

She sat down next to him and leaned in for a warm embrace. The keen expression in his eyes was the same, and dark hair framed his pale face. But hugging him was different. His bony frame felt thin and weak.

"How are you, Rolf? Our meetings haven't been the same without you," Soli said.

"What can I say? I'm a thirty year old with a worn-out body." He straightened. "Now, let's find our Heddy and the professor. I've had about enough of that German officer."

"So have we," Arvid said resolutely.

He and Birger moved two chairs closer to the coffee table, and Nikolai grabbed a kitchen stool and sat down at the end.

Rolf appeared more the intellectual type, perhaps a bit radical, but he never did anything haphazardly. He pushed the dark-rimmed glasses up on his nose. "Now, Nikolai and the boys have filled me in on everything that's happened in the last days. You've all been busy. I don't like the situation at all. Heddy has put herself in a dangerous place, first-handedly spying on Lieutenant Colonel Heinz Walter. It's all too close for comfort."

Soli was about to speak, but Rolf raised his hand and continued.

"That said...our Heddy is daring. No doubt about that. Under the circumstances and the sudden state of affairs at Professor Holst's office, she made a brave choice to help save him." He looked at Soli. "She wouldn't be able to help anyone if Walter had taken her away then... She might not even be alive." He cleared his voice. "Also, since we are in the secret business of preserving art from the enemy, I am thrilled about the Rembrandt painting of the musketeer. Soli and Heddy made good choices. There was no way you could have known Professor Holst's assistant would betray him and go to Walter with the information. I also agree with the decision to hide the artwork from the Ruber mansion on Oscar Street in Soli's secret room. Unless someone had the architectural drawings of her building and measured the size of the rooms in her basement, they'd never guess there's a hidden space down there. Normally, we'd take important artwork to Kongsberg and hide them in the silver mines, but with Heddy and the professor missing, we need Arvid and Birger here. Too much is at stake." Rolf leaned back and wiped his brow with a handkerchief. "Now, let's attack this situation from all angles and discuss where to go from here."

Arvid spoke first. "Birger and I have spent the day observing the entrances to Professor Holst's office and the Grand Hotel. We've patrolled the area around the crypt as well as the shop where Heddy's cousin works."

Birger added, "And we haven't seen Heddy at all. Either Walter keeps her in her room at the Grand, or she's not there any longer."

"But if she's not at the hotel, where could she be?" Soli asked. "Could she have run away? Maybe she's hiding somewhere…"

Nikolai hesitated. "Perhaps…but she would have contacted one of us. I've had a man on watch, too. He spotted Walter and his two closest men a few times but, unfortunately, no Heddy."

Rolf rubbed his chin. "So, with such little information, we don't have enough to create a detailed plan. If we started a cat-and-mouse-chase through our capital, we might attract unwanted attention."

Nikolai touched Soli's shoulder. "Walter must have plans for the painting. What options do you see?"

"Well, you would think he'd loot artwork for Hitler. There have been rumors in the art community that the

Führer wants to build an enormous art museum in Austria." She sighed. "Walter could also be wanting the Rembrandt as leverage to enforce his own power and influence in the Nazi hierarchy."

"As a gift or a bribe?" Birger asked.

"Maybe both. Giving the painting to Minister President Quisling or Reichskommisar Josef Terboven would no doubt strengthen Walter's position in Norway."

"But what do *you* think?" Rolf demanded.

Soli lifted her chin. "The times I've met Walter, he has seemed genuinely interested in classical artistry. He has never given me the impression of one who understands painting technique or even its history, but rather someone who enjoys beautiful, fine art. He may plan to keep the portrait for himself...hide it away from the world and just admire it. If I were him, that's what I'd do."

Suddenly, the doorhandle rattled in the hallway. Everyone froze.

"Are you expecting someone, Rolf?" Nikolai whispered.

Rolf shook his head in silence.

"Soli, go hide in the bedroom." Nikolai turned to Arvid and Birger. "You two stay by the kitchenette." He pulled his pistol out of his inner pocket, sneaked across the floor, and stood against the wall by the door.

Arvid offered to help Rolf somewhere else, but their host shook his head.

"I know you'll protect me, if necessary," Rolf said low.

Soli rushed into the bedroom but left the door slightly open to peek out.

The handle clattered once more—this time harder. Nikolai pointed his pistol at the door.

A sudden rap startled everyone in the room. A double knock, twice. Nikolai stared at Rolf, and the man simply shrugged. They were all present and not expecting anyone else.

Nikolai slowly turned the knob then took a step back, still pointing his weapon directly at the entrance.

Soli's muscles tightened. She rubbed her hands on her thighs. Who was at the door? Had they come this far, and now the Gestapo had found all of them cornered in one place? Her breath became quick and uneasy as the door opened.

A tall, fair-skinned man wearing a herringbone cap stepped inside and closed the door. He pulled his hat off, revealing a thick, blond mane.

Soli gasped then ran from the bedroom and jumped into his open arms.

"Sverre!"

He held her long then walked around the room, greeting each of his comrades.

"You can put your gun away now, Nikolai," Sverre said. "Some friend you are, pointing a weapon at me when I come home after months away." He gave Nikolai a bear hug and a manly pat on the back.

Rolf called out, "Come sit, everyone. Let's give the man a chance to explain why he's here."

Sverre sat down with Soli on the couch. "I'd love to tell you everything, but right now, I'm more concerned about finding Heddy."

"What do you know?" Rolf asked.

"Enough. I've been in town since yesterday and met a friend from Milorg who'd seen Heddy with Walter. So, I made some enquiries about where he was staying and kept watch outside the Grand Hotel. This morning, I saw Walter's two thugs drag her into a car and drive away. She didn't go with them voluntarily."

157

Soli gasped and covered her mouth.

"I didn't have a vehicle and felt totally useless... I stood there and watched them leave with her...a pistol pressed against her back. If only—"

Soli put her hand on Sverre's arm. "Wait... There's nothing you could have done then and there. Let's talk about what we can do now."

Sverre nodded. "I'm aware of that, but it was maddening. She looked my way, but I don't know if she recognized me through the car window. Since then, I've been running around, trying to find out where they were headed." He groaned. "I know those two goons. They gave me a good beating once." He spoke fast, not bothering to hide his anger.

Nikolai sat up. "Walter does not know our town and the surrounding area the way we do. He has a limited list of places he visits while he's here. It's time we run through that list. Where does Walter go? Which districts is he acquainted with? Then we narrow it down to where we think he could have had his men take Heddy."

Sverre ran his fingers through his hair. "I've had those same thoughts, Nikolai, and I've narrowed it down to one area."

"Where?" Arvid asked.

"Sorkedalen," Sverre replied. "The Germans have a few cabins out there. It's a secluded place on the outskirts of town. No one will look for her out there."

"It would be extremely risky for any of you to go there. You'd be trespassing in their territory," Rolf said, shaking his head.

Oblivious to the danger involved, Sverre lifted his chin and stated firmly, "They've taken something of ours. We're just going there to take it back."

No one protested. They all knew Sverre well. Once he'd made up his mind, he gave everything. During the war, that had gotten him into trouble many times.

Birger shifted in his seat. "There's more."

Sverre gave him a stern look. "Tell me."

Arvid explained. "Walter has also kidnapped Soli's old archaeology professor and stolen a Rembrandt painting."

Sverre smacked his forehead. "So that's what this is all about. I'd only heard one of my Milorg friends had seen Heddy with Walter. Now I understand why. This is typical of Heddy...putting herself in harm's way to save someone else."

"The same as you do, Sverre," Rolf said with a crooked smile. "We're all so grateful to have you back. Now, let's discuss how to find Heddy, Professor Holst, and, hopefully, the Rembrandt painting."

Soli stared at Sverre, studying his handsome profile. Her big brother was back. Right there...close enough for Soli to hug him. She was elated to have him in Oslo. On the other hand, she was terrified someone would recognize him. The last time the Gestapo caught him, Sverre barely survived their torture.

She leaned closer and whispered, "You know Heddy would never—"

"I know, Soli. Heddy is playing a role, being the brave and enduring woman that she is. I'm so proud of her but at the same time beyond myself with worry."

"Me, too, Sverre." She gave him a concerned look. "Where have you been staying since you came back? You need to come to the shop and sleep in my secret room downstairs."

He shook his head. "I've been hiding in a shed the last

two nights, but I thought I'd ask Rolf if I can have his couch tonight."

Rolf nodded. "Of course."

Soli started to protest. She wanted her brother close. "But—"

"Little sister, I don't want anyone to see me walking in and out of your place. This is a crowded part of town with lots of apartment buildings where I can blend in easily with the rest of the men coming and going. I'll stay here tonight, then we'll take it from there."

Rolf clapped. "Now, everyone. I say we start our operation tomorrow early afternoon and have several pickup points on our way out of town. Dressed as factory workers, we'll follow the stream of buses and cars leaving town after the first shift."

"What about the checkpoints on the north side toward the valley?" Arvid asked.

"They set up roadblocks there from time to time, so have your identification papers handy, just in case." Rolf patted Soli on the arm. "Could you get some glasses and a pitcher of water? I may have some crackers, too. Planning the details may take a while."

Nikolai stroked Soli's hand as she passed on her way to the kitchen. "You need to keep your shop open as normal tomorrow morning. Too many closed days might seem suspicious."

She beamed a subtle smile his way. "Yes, what doesn't seem suspicious?"

TUESDAY, 1 MAY 1945

CHAPTER SIXTEEN

CABIN IN SORKEDALEN

AFTER A FEW HOURS of drifting in and out of sleep, worrying and analyzing everything and nothing, Heddy watched a pale light seep through the windowpane. She got up from the floor and wrapped the woolen blanket around the professor. She walked to the window and wound up her wristwatch. Five. Still early.

Coughing, Professor Holst started moving. "Heddy?"

"Good morning, Professor."

He coughed again. "Do you see anything out there?"

"No, but the sky is blue. It'll be a lovely spring day. We'll get out there soon. I promise. Maybe we'll even find some food in the kitchen upstairs."

The professor got to his feet, poured some more water in the cup, and handed half a piece of dry bread to Heddy. "There's not much food left, but we can share the rest of this and hope for the best. It will give us a little strength."

Heddy swallowed the bread and had a sip of water before she scrambled up the stairs and continued hammering at the basement door. She had to break it open before the men returned to pick up the painting. And since Walter had decided he didn't need her or the professor anymore, she had to find a way out. They'd grab the painting from the attic and vanish into the surrounding woodland before the lieutenant colonel and his men showed up. She was not about to die in a deserted cabin.

After a few more hours of smashing the hammer against the wood, the security device finally broke.

Pushing the door open, Heddy called out, "We need to find the painting and escape from here. Do you need help getting up the stairs?"

"I can manage. You go first."

Holst climbed the steps and followed Heddy onto the main floor. The morning sun shone through the windows and gave the room a golden glow. To her surprise, it was a quaint little cabin. A kitchen counter was straight ahead, and a table and chairs stood off to the right. An open door revealed a small room with two sets of bunk beds.

"Where's the trapdoor to the attic?"

"It's here," Professor Holst said and pointed to the ceiling.

"Good. The rod to open the latch should be right here somewhere."

The wooden pole hung on a nail next to the front entrance.

"I found it." Heddy grabbed the rod and raised it up to unhook the clasp. Suddenly, she stopped.

"What's wrong?" the professor asked.

"There's a car coming."

She ran to the kitchen window and peeked behind the curtains. "Oh, no. They're back already. They can't find us up here. I'm sorry, Professor, but we need to pretend we're still locked up." She replaced the rod on the hook and guided the professor back to the basement door. "Climb back down. I'll try to attach the padlock on the chain. It won't be right, but with any luck, those men will be too busy to notice it's broken."

Holst stepped onto the top of the stairs. "Hurry, Heddy. I hear them, too, now. They only need a minute to remove the wire, but as soon as that's done, they'll barge in here."

"You'd better hurry downstairs," she whispered. "Tread carefully. Those stairs are far from safe."

She replaced the broken padlock on the chain and hung it loosely in front of the basement closure. Then she crawled through the narrow crack and pulled the door shut. Barely breathing, she sat on the top step, trying to eavesdrop. The front door opened. Stomping boots moved across the floor. She put a finger to her lips to let the professor know the enemy had entered the cabin.

Something was different...only two voices were there, discussing in German. Didn't Walter return with the men? What did that mean? Had the soldiers come back alone to finish off their prisoners?

"The boss is at the farm eating a delectable meal while we're running his errands. Did you see that place? The enormous manor, red barn and stables, and two *stabbur*?" The thin soldier with the high-pitched voice sounded irritated.

The sturdy guard answered, "Yeah, quite impressive. And the roof? Glazed black tiles. I tell you; only wealthy people can afford something like that—even before the war."

"I know, and here we are...sleeping in barracks or in small, cheap rooms as we travel back and forth between

Germany and Norway with the *Obersturmbannführer*. It's not fair. Aren't you tired of being pushed around by him sometimes, not taking part in any of the good meals and comfortable lifestyle? How did he get to receive such a high military rank, anyway? I have a decent education, but I'm stuck here doing his bidding."

"I hear you. The *Obersturmbannführer* showed bravery during a siege and planned an attack on the enemy early on during the war, or so I've been told. That's how he was decorated with those ribbons and aiguillettes he flaunts so proudly. But I can't imagine him ever getting his hands dirty." The man's hoarse voice had a disgusted tone. He was clearly not satisfied with their commanding officer.

"It must have been his courage in an office, comfortably scheduling projects around a table that gave him his medals. Luckily for him, that first blockade went well."

They both burst into loud guffaws.

"Ha-ha, probably true that," the sturdy soldier said. "Easy to be brave when you stand in a comfortable room, a drink in one hand, planning what others have to do." He paused then continued. "I have a mind to tell his superiors what he's up to. I mean, how long have we backed him now, and all he does is look for ways to become rich, all under the pretense of finding art for the Führer."

"I agree, my friend. Life is not fair for the likes of us. Come, let's finish this."

Someone picked the rod from the wall and started opening the attic latch.

"What are we going to do about the old man? Are we taking him, too?" the thin soldier asked.

"No, we were to leave him here for now. Our commander and Haraldsen have probably finished their early lunch at the villa. We need to hurry over there with the artwork so the lieutenant colonel can finalize the sale. You know him. He has the patience of a fly."

"*Jawohl*. You get the painting from the attic, and I'll get the girl."

Heddy's pulse raised. She had no place to hide but grabbed the hammer, clutching it until her knuckles went white. She would not let the soldiers take her away without a fight. And what about the Rembrandt? The portrait had been within their grasp only minutes ago. Where were the men taking it?

Holst stood in the middle of the basement floor, wide-eyed, waiting to hear what was going on upstairs. How could she tell him the men were coming for her?

The hoarse soldier burst out. "No! The lock's broken. If those two have escaped, Walter will punish us from here to China."

The other man yelled from the attic, "You *Dummkopf*! Go check on them. And if they're gone, we'll find them. They won't get far in these woods."

Heddy stood behind the door, the hammer raised, ready to hit whoever came through. Her heart beat faster with every rustle and jingle of the chain on the other side of the door. Before she knew it, the door flew open. She lifted her hand higher to strike, but the sturdy soldier grabbed her arm, jerked the hammer out of her grasp, and tossed it across the floor. No matter how much she struggled, he tugged her up the last step and through the door. He held her with one arm while turning the key.

"What about the professor?" Heddy yelled.

"Quiet, woman. We don't care about him."

The thin man climbed down the ladder from the attic and placed the crate professor Holst had built on the floor. "She's trouble, but we have to get the painting to the

Obersturmbannführer right away," he hissed. "Our orders were to get rid of her."

"Your lieutenant colonel only uses you," Heddy yelled. "Stand up for yourselves. Choose. Free the professor and let us both go."

The sturdy soldier smacked Heddy on her cheek. "Stop talking," he said brusquely. He turned to his mate. "Put the painting in the trunk of the car. We'll dump her on the way there."

Heddy kept wiggling, trying to get out of the man's grasp. "That painting is stolen. Rise above Walter's ridiculous orders and do the right thing."

"I told you to hush." The man raised his arm and brought it down on Heddy's head.

She sank to the floor and blacked out.

CHAPTER SEVENTEEN

OSLO, NORWAY

SOLI HADN'T RESTED well during the night. Every time she drifted off to sleep, frantic dreams about Heddy and Sverre in danger played in her head. Seeing her best friend at the café on Sunday had calmed Soli's fear, but only momentarily. Now that Sverre relentlessly roamed the streets of Oslo, and Walter's men had abducted Heddy at gunpoint taking her goodness knew where, Soli's bad habit of making up horrible scenarios spiraled out of control.

Half an hour before her shop opened, Soli sat downstairs in her secret room, yawning. To calm her thoughts, she went through the prints and drawings from the Ruber residence. She longed for the Rembrandt, too. Only to study it. What an adventurous story that painting could tell, having been lost for about three hundred years. They had to get it back and eventually help the portrait find its way home to the descendants of its original owner. Reuniting a painting with the right person gave Soli an indescribable satisfaction. Other people might think it strange, but to her, it was almost like bringing two family members together after a long time apart.

The wall clock struck nine in her office on the main floor. Soli locked the secret room, pushed the bookshelf to hide the door, and went upstairs to open the shop.

As she unlocked the front door, a customer was already waiting outside.

"Good morning." She rubbed her arms. "Please come inside. It's a bit nippy out there."

Carrying a paper-wrapped package, the old man entered the showroom. "I was eager to show you a painting my sister gave me."

She invited him to take a seat in the comfortable chair in the corner of the room and moved the art history books from the table to the floor. "Just put your artwork here. Let's look at what you have."

He meticulously untied the string and unwrapped the parcel. "My sister says it's valuable. I find it quite modern...but I like it. What do you think?"

The interpretation of a few dishes on a kitchen counter with a window in the background resembled artwork from the turn of the century. Soli recognized the Fauvist style with its non-naturalistic depictions and daring, textured brushstrokes used by French artists like Matisse and Cézanne. At least the Germans wouldn't steal this painting. Hitler had set a standard early on that expressionistic art was degenerate and radical. The Reich's art promotion was all about romantic realism. Soli loved both styles and found it infuriating that the Führer thought he could control people's opinion of art movements—that he could restrict the free will to choose.

She tilted her head. "Well, it's similar to works by our own Ludvig Karsten who favored bold colors, especially cobalt blue like in this picture. I think this artist tried to recreate Ludvig Karsten's *The Blue Kitchen* from 1913. This painting was done by an amateur, but the most important thing is that you enjoy the composition, the hues, and the feeling you get when you look at it."

The old man relaxed in the soft chair and folded his arms. "I do like it. The scene takes me back to my childhood."

Soli smiled. "Then you should absolutely keep it."

The gentleman got up and shook her hand. "Thank you. Could you make a suitable frame for it?"

"I can do that. Should I show you some examples of different framework? The selection is somewhat limited now...you understand. And perhaps you want the frame to match other things on your wall."

The old man shook his head. "No. I leave all that up to you. I trust your judgment."

He bid her good day then left. His visit to the shop had been a pleasant diversion, a relief from Soli's worries. But as soon as she was on her own again, her muscles tensed. A few more hours of work then she'd close early and meet the boys.

Nikolai came by around half an hour later.

"I wanted to see you, but I only have two minutes," he said and handed her a small bouquet of pink roses and daisies from the florist.

"I'm so glad you chose to spend those few seconds with me."

Oh, how she adored this good man. Soli placed the flowers on the table then stood on her tiptoes and gently rubbed her nose against his. When their lips softly met, he tightened his grip around her shoulders, and everything else vanished. She clung to him as if letting go would mean the end of the world.

He eased his hold but kept her close. "I'm sorry, Soli. My time is up, and work is calling."

"I understand. Thank you for the flowers." She opened the door for him. "Until later, then. I can't wait to thwart Walter's plans, whatever they are."

"We all want to stop him." He planted a last kiss on her cheek. "See you in a couple of hours."

Soli stood by the window until he turned the corner and disappeared out of view. She picked up the art history books, arranged them on the table, and put the flowers in a water-filled vase and set them in the middle.

Around lunchtime, Walter's two men who'd waited for Heddy outside the café by the harbor passed Soli's shop. They stopped in front of her display window for a moment then continued down the street.

Her mouth went dry. They had to be the same soldiers who'd forced Heddy into a car outside the hotel. What if they returned with the lieutenant colonel? How could she possibly hide the fact she'd spoken with Heddy, and she knew he had the musketeer painting? Could she keep quiet about Sverre having seen Walter's men kidnap her best friend? Or what if that brute interrogated her about the covert plan she'd concocted with the boys?

Trying not to worry was easier said than done. At least, Sverre had the sense to stay away from her shop. Soli kept busy. She sold an etching to a German couple then worked on the old man's frame. Twice more she noticed Walter's men—one time across the street, standing by a lamp post, smoking, the other time strolling casually by the window, glancing in. She gulped down air, as if they could hear her breathing. Undeniably, she did not want to confront them right now. She didn't have the strength.

One customer asked for help with a broken frame that had slipped off a nail on the wall.

"It's a good thing the artwork is intact. I can't see any damage to the etching. The frame I can repair," Soli said.

The client seemed satisfied. As the man left, Walter's two men passed him in the doorway and entered the shop. It was inevitable. They'd kept her under surveillance for the last hour or two.

"Guten Tag." The sturdy man spoke with a raspy voice.

Soli curtsied. "Good day. What may I help you with?"

The soldiers didn't answer but walked around her showroom, staring at the pictures on the wall as if they were seriously interested in making a purchase. After several rounds, they nodded and strode toward the front door.

"*Danke schön, Fräulein,*" the other man said and closed the door behind them.

She sat down. *Breathe, Soli. Don't let them rock you.*

As she caught her breath, Soli heard a knock on her back door. She hurried to open.

Arvid and Birger stood outside.

"Are you ready to close the store?" Arvid asked.

"Yes, absolutely. I can hardly wait to get away from here. Walter's men have been watching my shop all afternoon. I hope they didn't see you."

"Nah, there was no one there," Birger said. "Why are they checking up on you?"

Arvid frowned. "I don't like it. If Walter wanted artwork for his new second home on Oscar Street, he would have come himself and asked you for help in picking out suitable paintings."

Soli nodded. "I agree. Why have they been sneaking around corners the last few hours, observing my shop as if I'm under suspicion for some criminal act?"

"We should leave right away. I'll go out front and make sure the coast is clear," Arvid said.

Birger shifted his feet, his eyes darting nervously. "I'll go. Look for me in the alley across the street. I'll put my hands in my pockets when it's safe for us to go together." He turned and hurried outside.

Soli rushed through the showroom and locked the front exit. She checked that the door to the basement was thoroughly secured, then she grabbed her purse and walked out the back door with Arvid, turning the key before they left.

Arvid peeked around the side of the building. "Our boy is indicating it's safe to go now."

"Good." She took long strides to keep up with Arvid. "Are we still meeting Nikolai and Sverre at the harbor?"

"No, we should split up. There are too many German soldiers out on the streets today. I'll go to Aker Harbor, and you and our boy here will meet us farther down by the mechanical factory at Piper Cove. You go first, then Birger will follow. Now, hurry!"

*

Twenty minutes later, Soli stood with Birger on a quiet corner of Holmen's Street. The truck drove up, and Arvid, Sverre, and Nikolai jumped out.

Sverre gathered everyone close. "Listen, I met our friend Z this morning. She'd just received an encrypted message from London. Adolf Hitler was found dead yesterday. They announced it in Germany today."

Birger grinned. "Great news! Good riddance to the

HEIDI ELJARBO

dictator. Has anyone seen any newspaper articles about it?"

"I check several papers every day at the police station, but there was nothing this morning about Hitler being dead. The paper, *Adresseavisa*, confirmed that *National Samling*, the Norwegian Nazi party, were victorious," Nikolai said.

Arvid flipped his hand. "Bah! It's ridiculous how that party gags the press. They even change newspaper headings or remove the papers altogether."

Soli stood in shock for a moment, letting the news sink in, thoughts frantically running circles in her head. Could it really be true?

"How did he die?" she finally asked.

Sverre was unfolding the tarpaulin on the bed of the truck. "Suicide...but I don't know all the details yet." He opened the passenger door for Soli.

She climbed in. "What happens now?"

"No idea, but we still have several hundred thousand German soldiers in our country, and even though this may be the last sting for the Reich, it may take a while to get rid of them."

Nikolai jumped up next to Soli. "We need to go."

"I'll drive," Arvid said and got in behind the steering wheel. "Just pray we'll make it out of town."

Sverre and Birger pushed tools, rope, and knives out of the way and lay down on the truck bed, covering themselves with the tarpaulin. They knocked on the back of the cabin to indicate they were ready, and Arvid steered the vehicle onto the west highway out of town. Ten minutes up the road, he turned right toward Ullern and the valley going north from Roa.

For once, they were not stopped by roadblocks. The

roads seemed strangely quiet. Had people heard the reports from Berlin? Did their German occupants know what had happened? And if they did, how would the announcement about their Führer's suicide affect their behavior?

"Unfortunately, I don't think news about Hitler changes Walter's goals," Soli said.

Nikolai took hold of her hand. "I'm sure you're right about that."

They drove past the residential area north of Roa and into the country. The golf course at Bogstad was still a ploughed field, something the owners had done at the beginning of the war to prevent the enemy from enjoying their leisure time there. Only a few green patches were left, enough for local youngsters to play nine holes.

They entered the valley. Farms were far apart, and dark woods hugged the narrow road on both sides. They sat in silence, distressed by the solemn rescue mission before them and the fact that they didn't know if Heddy was still alive.

Soli sat staring out the side window at the passing scenery when something caught her eye. *What was that?* A sudden feeling of cold rushed through her body. Certain she'd seen someone lying in the ditch a short way back, she yelled, "Stop the car!"

Arvid hit the brakes. "What did you see?"

"There was someone in the ditch next to the road. It looked like—"

Sverre jumped off the back and ran to the person lying there. By the time Soli and the others joined him, he'd picked up Heddy from the cold ground and enfolded her in his arms.

"Oh, my darling. What have they done to you?" he said

softly, cradling her as a baby, holding her close as if he'd never let go.

"She must be cold." Soli removed her coat and placed it around Heddy's shoulders. "Here."

Heddy slowly opened her eyes. Her body trembled, and she couldn't seem to control her chattering teeth.

"Heddy, darling, have you been here long?" Sverre asked.

"I don't know," she answered. "The last thing I remember was that Walter's men came back to the cabin to pick up the painting. I'd become a burden, and Walter had told them to do away with me. They must have hit me over the head because I don't recall anything else. Then I woke up here."

Soli stroked her cheek. "Do you know what time of day they came?"

Heddy wrapped her arms tightly around herself to control the shivers. "It wasn't dark when they picked me up... It must have been a few hours ago."

Sverre carefully pulled back her hair.

"Is it bad?" Heddy asked. "My head hurts something horrible."

"You'll be fine," he answered. "Some dried blood and a good-sized bump on your head."

"We should take a look at that bump," Soli said.

Heddy shook her head. "No, no...we must get the professor first."

Birger moved closer. "The professor?"

"Yes, Holst is in the cabin. At least, he was there. We need to hurry."

Sverre looked up at the others. "We need to pick up the professor then find Walter. It's time to deal with that man once and for all."

"Walter went to see someone...to make a deal," Heddy said.

Arvid stepped forward. "What kind of deal? Where?"

"His men talked about a rich buyer farther up the valley."

Soli gasped. "He's selling the Rembrandt painting of the musketeer."

Heddy nodded slowly. "Yes, they must have come to an agreement because the soldiers came back for the portrait. For some reason, they'd been told to get rid of me in the process."

"Oh, how could they?" Soli carefully smoothed Heddy's hair. "We're just grateful we found you."

"Me, too," Heddy whispered.

"You're safe now, my darling," Sverre said. "I'm not leaving you alone as long as that man is in the country."

"What about the guards? Will they return to the cabin again today?" Birger asked.

Heddy gave him a blank look. "Sorry...I don't know. They're probably running errands for Walter, but we need to be careful in case they come back."

Heddy tried to stand but staggered back.

"I've got you." Sverre carefully seized Heddy and lifted her up in his arms.

"Sit up front with her," Nikolai said. "It's warmer there." He waved at Soli and the boys. "Come on, everyone."

While Sverre carried Heddy to the front seat, Soli jumped on the back with the others. Nikolai removed his jacket and placed it around her shoulders.

She snuggled closer. "I recognize this area. This is where they kept Sverre locked up last year. Heddy and I were here, hiding in the bushes, and someone chased us through the woods. It was horrible."

"Walter was here, too, wasn't he?" Birger asked.

"Yes, and he knows what Sverre stands for. Heddy and I managed to stay hidden until he'd left."

Arvid turned right onto a gravel road that took them to a red cabin with a shed on the side. It looked deserted, no cars or other signs of anyone there. He parked behind a cluster of trees, out of sight from the street below, and they all scrambled out.

"Never thought I'd come back here." Sverre rubbed his hands. "Birger, Arvid...you two go around to the other side. Nikolai, check the shed. Heddy and Soli, come with me to the entrance."

Heddy grabbed Sverre's arm. "Wait. Two of the doors are wired."

"Oh, no. I'll tell the everyone." He ran after the other men around the corner.

Heddy set out in the opposite direction.

"Where are you going?" Soli followed her to the north end the cottage.

Kneeling outside a narrow window, Heddy looked in. "I have to tell him we're here." She knocked vigorously on the windowpane.

Soli crouched beside her and peeked through the glass. Holst was inside, smiling weakly but waving back. He started coughing and sat down, pressing a hand to his chest. Soli put her arm around Heddy. The professor was alive, and soon, they'd free him from captivity.

Sverre came up behind them. "Is he there?"

Heddy nodded. "Yes, he'll need some care and nourishment to be nursed back to health, but he's still with us.

Sverre, hurry…get him out of there. Walter and his men tend to show up unexpectedly."

"All right. We'll check with Nikolai and the boys. In one way or another, we'll get through that door."

They hurried back to the front of the cabin.

Arvid stood with his arms crossed. "You're right, Heddy. We checked the entrances. The main door and the basement door both have explosives attached to the handle, and the windows have extra bolted locks."

"What kind of explosives?" Nikolai asked.

Birger chewed his lip. "Enough to hurt a man badly."

Arvid's face tightened. "But why the safety measures way out here? I mean, it's just a small cottage in the woods."

"Because this is where Walter keeps his personal prisoners… I was one of them once." Sverre walked closer to the door and studied the contraption.

"And Walter's stolen art," Heddy said. "His lootings are in the attic."

"Ah, interesting. We're unraveling all his secrets one by one." Sverre strode to the truck and checked the supplies they'd brought. "Which could we remove faster —the explosives on the doors or one of the bolted windows?"

Nikolai pursed his lips. "I'd say the explosives…that is, if someone knows how to do it properly. I've had some training with bombs at work, but I'm no expert."

"There must be an easy way to do it," Heddy said. "Walter and his men come and go here all the time."

"I'll do it," Birger said and took a step forward. He had a determined look on his young face. "When I was arrested last year, I sat in a cell with a couple of guys who discussed these sorts of explosive traps all the time. I picked up some pointers."

Soli walked up to him. "But, Birger, are you sure? We don't want you to get hurt."

He grinned. "Yeah, I'm sure. Did we bring some pliers?"

Nikolai put his hand on Soli's back and gently pushed her behind the truck.

"He'll be all right, won't he?" she asked with a tremor in her voice.

"There's much more to Birger than his optimistic attitude. He's one of the bravest men I know." Nikolai gave her hand a comforting squeeze.

Soli leaned her head on Nikolai's shoulder, closed her eyes, and said a silent prayer for Birger's safety. The fear of losing her nearest friends had often overpowered her. They'd been through so much together and were such a close-knit group. She couldn't imagine her life without any single one of them.

Within seconds, Birger turned around with an elated smile on his face. "It's safe, thanks to my mates in the prison cell who discussed explosive devices and weapons day in and day out."

Sverre opened the door. "Show the way, Heddy."

She entered first and went straight to the basement door. A trunk blocked the entrance.

"The men must have been in a hurry," she said. "They didn't take time to put the chains and padlock back in place."

Nikolai and Arvid lifted the trunk out of the way, and Heddy swung the door open.

"Professor Holst, we're coming," she called out.

The old man stood at the bottom of the stairs. Nikolai

rushed down and helped the professor up the rickety steps. The professor wobbled a bit, and his face was ashen and drawn in a look of malnutrition and discomfort.

He stared at the wound on her head. "What did they do to you, child? I'm sorry I wasn't strong enough to help you more."

"Don't worry about me. I'll be fine."

Holst then stretched a hand toward Soli. "And you, my young student, without your knowledge and expertise, we wouldn't have known how important that painting was."

They were in enemy territory and marked by the horror of Walter's violence, but for a moment, Soli felt a relief of bodily tension that had built up during the last days. Standing there among dear friends, her brother, her Nikolai...holding the professor's feeble hand...she welcomed a comforting calmness. Grateful the professor was well, Soli blinked back tears. A few drops escaped, and she wiped her cheek. Heinz Walter walked over corpses to get his hands on profitable artwork. Even though Soli's passion for art history often filled her very being, it was never fueled by greed.

As they turned to leave, Sverre caught Soli gazing up at the attic latch. In the middle of all the fear, she found a twinkle of amusement. She passed him a wry smile.

"I'm very curious about what Walter has stashed up there," she said. "But we can return later. First, we need to locate the Rembrandt painting."

"You're a smart little sister," Sverre said. He squeezed her arm. "Come on. Let's go get your musketeer portrait."

CHAPTER EIGHTEEN

SORKEDALEN, NORWAY

IT WAS DARK by the time Soli and her resistance group gathered by the truck. Heddy sat on a rock, fingering her necklace, and Soli put her arm around her friend.

"Do you remember the last conversation you over-heard before the guards took you away?" Soli asked.

"Walter's men spoke of a stately farm farther up the valley." Heddy rubbed a hand on the back of her neck. "It has a white house with glazed black tiles. And there was a name...Haraldsen. Yes, that was it."

Professor Holst held up his finger. "I know that place. Actually, it's an old parsonage. Pastor Haraldsen joined the Nazi party at the beginning of the war. He keeps a low profile, but rumor has it he's made a formidable profit during the last years. No one I've talked to knows how."

Nikolai shoved his hands into his pockets. "You think he's been collaborating with Walter?"

Heddy nodded. "I do. The lieutenant colonel doesn't want to take the artwork to Germany. He wants to get rich by stealing and dealing."

"Haraldsen hasn't performed many sermons the last years, only for Easter and Christmas and other such days that are part of the liturgical season. The chapel is small and old. The parishioners meet in a church closer to Oslo."

Holst coughed a bit, and Birger stepped up and held his arm for support.

Sverre adjusted his herringbone cap. "So, the pastor's had time to work on his extracurricular activities...like collecting stolen art."

Heddy nodded again. "I'm afraid that's what it looks like."

Soli ran back inside the cabin and grabbed three woolen blankets from the bedroom. She returned and handed one to Heddy. "Here...you and the professor need to stay warm."

Sverre clapped. "All right, people. Everyone in the truck. Heddy, you sit up front with the professor and Arvid. The rest of you...climb onto the back. Let's go find this place."

They followed the valley northward, searching for a large farm with a white manor and a small church. Soli sat next to Nikolai, holding his hand. Professor Holst had mentioned that Pastor Haraldsen was a peculiar art collector and was somewhat of a loner. But they had no idea what was ahead. Walter could still be there with his two assailants. Or what if the pastor had invited a group from the Nazi elite to discuss what to do about stolen art now that the war was coming to an end? Sverre sat with eyes closed. He most likely hadn't slept much the last nights. It was good to have him close again, but how far would his daring heroism take him once they arrived at the parsonage?

Nikolai nudged Soli's shoulder. "What's wrong? You seem tense…and unnaturally quiet."

"I'm just a bit nervous. What will happen when we get there? The pastor could be a trained gunman. He could have guards around his property."

"We don't know anything yet, so let's put off worrying until we get there. We may not even be able to find the painting."

"I know. And I'm trying to prepare myself for that, but my hope is to bring justice to the Rembrandt and the Ruber family who are the rightful owners." She straightened her back. "At least, we'll try our best."

"That's all we can do."

Heddy knocked on the rear window and pointed up the hill.

Birger leaned over the right edge of the truck. "Lights up ahead. There are several buildings and a church steeple above the treetops."

Soli stretched her neck. The glow of a white moon lit up the landscape enough to see the silhouette of the farm and a small chapel.

"That must be the place," Nikolai said. "Do you boys have your weapons ready?"

Sverre patted his pocket. "I have a pistol, and Birger has his rifle."

"Good. You know what to do."

The truck's headlights were already masked to reduce light. Arvid turned them completely off before they reached the farm. He steered the car onto the side of the road and switched off the engine.

Nikolai hopped off the back and helped Soli down. "Keep low. We don't know what awaits us up there."

Birger found a long, straight, stout stick and handed it to the professor. "Here…something to steady your steps."

The professor cupped his hand on Birger's shoulder. "Thank you, young man. This is just what I need. I may be weak now, but I've survived this far and certainly don't want to miss this quest."

Noticing how Holst struggled, Soli turned back.

"Professor, I know you'd like to come, but how about you wait in the car? We'll tell you everything afterward."

"You're right, dear Soli. My legs don't have the strength to carry me any farther."

She helped him onto the seat, removed the walking stick, and enveloped him in the blanket. "We'll be back soon."

He placed his hand on hers and nodded. "Be careful."

She hurried after the others. Soft, flickering lights came from the elongated, stained-glass church windows. A grove of naked birch trees stood in silent parade around the back part. Other than that, the main house and other building lay in darkness, probably well covered by protective blackout shades on the windows. Was it a farm or a parsonage? It seemed to be a combination but didn't show traces of any animals. Maybe it had been a thriving ranch once. Had the Germans depleted the livestock, or was the pastor simply not interested in agriculture and raising barn creatures?

They huddled together as a small band, crouching, moving forward a little at a time, with their gazes darting between the buildings up ahead and the immediate vicinity. Soli held Heddy's hand, supporting her when she needed it. Arvid had tried to convince Heddy to wait by the truck, but she wouldn't hear of it. Sverre had allowed her to join them, on condition she'd stay in the rear and throw herself to the ground if they had to hide fast. Heddy didn't protest, a sure sign she was unwell and willing to leave the tough decisions to others.

"I don't see Walter's car anywhere?" Arvid whispered.

Sverre said, "No, but there's a vehicle parked by the barn. Maybe it belongs to the pastor. What do you think, Nikolai?"

"It seems awfully quiet. The lieutenant colonel is probably long gone by now. We'll check the Grand Hotel again when we return to Oslo." Nikolai turned to Soli. "We need evidence before we can approach Haraldsen. If the Rembrandt painting is here, where would the pastor keep it?"

"As an avid collector, he'd either display the artwork in his home, or he could have a special room or gallery dedicated to his collections." Soli kept her eyes on the chapel. "I want to check the church first. There's a light on in there. Haraldsen is busy with something...and from what the professor said earlier, the pastor doesn't spend much time preparing sermons."

"All right." Sverre raised his hand and motioned for them to move forward to the chapel.

As they drew nearer, they noticed the whitewashed building had tar-stained wooden gables.

"This has been here for centuries," Soli whispered. "It could have been a proprietary chapel."

"What does that mean?" Heddy asked.

"That the church belonged to a private individual. This does not look like your normal parsonage. There are only a few gravestones among the birch trees. If we studied the names engraved, we might find generations from the same family."

"Hmm, that could explain why Haraldsen only gives a

few sermons a year."

Arvid had run ahead to check if someone was inside. He returned, shaking his head. "Looks safe, but the pastor is bound to return soon. The door was slightly ajar, and dim lights on the side walls are lit."

Soli slipped through the pointed arch door first. A single candelabra holding five half-burned candles sparkled like a beacon on a lace-covered table, giving the vestibule an antiquated feeling. She was about to move through the narrow narthex and into the central nave when Birger stuck his head in and whispered low.

"He's coming back, Soli. You need to get out."

She turned and glanced through the open crack in the door. It was already too late. The man whistled as he crossed the yard, wiping his mouth as if he'd just finished his supper. Nikolai knocked on a small window, waving at her to leave, but Soli shook her head. She stretched to see if there might be a side door in the back of the sanctuary, but she simply didn't have enough time to explore the possibilities. Without hesitation, she ran up the stairs to the gallery above the narthex. Pressing her back against the wall by the organ, she squeezed her elbows into her sides, making her body as small as possible.

Surveying the nave down below, she widened her eyes. Pastor Haraldsen—or should she call him an art collector—had dozens of paintings lined up along the aisle against the side of the pews. Some artwork hung on the brick walls between the few stained-glass windows, and the altar was also used as a stand. It was a most amazing gallery of beautiful art, but where was the Rembrandt?

The door shut. He was in the church...alone with Soli. Nikolai and her friends were outside. Although the fear of being detected seized her quivering body, she was more than curious to see what Haraldsen was up to. The man was clearly unconventional...and strange. Soli had no doubt she was about to observe something bizarre and treacherous.

She squeezed the sides of her pants when he came into view below. Haraldsen looked like a thin fifty year old with a receding hairline and slick strands of hair combed toward the back of his head to hide bald spots. He seemed content, slowly strolling up the aisle with his hands clasped behind his back, humming. Now and then, he stopped to caress various paintings. He even spoke to the artwork as if they were pets or loved ones.

Suddenly, Soli held her hand over her mouth so as not to gasp out loud. There in the chancel at the altar was the portrait by Rembrandt. Haraldsen stood in front of the altar, staring at the baroque rendition for a moment, speaking low. She couldn't make out the words, but it sounded as if he was bidding the musketeer goodnight.

Why didn't he hide the paintings somewhere safer? What kind of precaution had he taken to keep thieves and unauthorized people away? His business with Walter was kept private, no doubt about that, and from what Professor Holst had said, the pastor didn't entertain guests much. It was in Walter's own interest to let Haraldsen maintain his solitary life. That way, the two men could continue their illicit trading.

How much of a hermit was Haraldsen? Had any of her colleagues ever met him? Soli had never heard his name mentioned in her art community. Either they didn't know the pastor, or they were part of his shady business. In the years she'd been involved in the art world, she'd never picked up anything about the old church full of art. Haraldsen must have operated under a false name and executed his underhanded transactions without contracts or legal certificates.

Soli did not have the impression Haraldsen purchased and sold art only to make a profit. This was an extreme collector, and people like that had a passion for the pieces in their possession. But that was where Haraldsen and Soli differed. She would never collect stolen paintings unto herself. And she'd never deal in obscure secrecy with Nazi leaders to obtain such art treasures. Yes, Haraldsen appeared wealthy, but the man most likely enjoyed the satisfaction of admiring old renditions, knowing he owned artwork no one else had. Who would look for precious art in such an old church, anyway?

Soli waited until Haraldsen had made his rounds. He snuffed all the candles in the vestibule and left, closing the door behind him. When she heard the key turn in the lock, she realized she'd been locked inside.

She tiptoed down the stairs, opened a tiny side window, and whispered into the night. "Are you out there? He locked up, and I don't have a key."

Nikolai snuck up under the open pane. "See if you can find another one. Sometimes, a spare key is kept in the outer hall or an office."

She hurried into the hallway and fumbled about. She couldn't turn the lights back on, but the moon shone through the small vestibule window. In the vestibule, she found a couple of keys in a drawer. She tried the first one without any luck. The second key was a match. She opened the door and led everyone into the nave.

Nikolai lit a match. "So many paintings. Haraldsen has been at this business for a long time."

"Let's just get the one we're after for now," Sverre said. "Soli, do you know where your Rembrandt is?"

"It's by the altar."

He gave her an understanding look and stroked her cheek. "I know that look, little sister. You wish you had the time to check every painting in here. I promise, we'll try to find out about the rest later, all right? We'll get this man. He's played a role in a criminal act, dealing in stolen goods and collaborating with the Gestapo. Once the war is over, men like him will be punished severely."

Soli nodded. "Yes, Sverre, I know. Haraldsen's not about to part with any of these paintings soon. He spoke to them as if they were his children."

Heddy scanned the room. "I don't see the crate for the painting anywhere."

"There's no time to look for it now. We need to just take it as it is." Sverre pointed to a sheet that hung across the front pew.

"It's not ideal, but it'll do," Soli said. "We should hide the Rembrandt in my secret room until we figure out what to do about it."

Arvid wrapped the Rembrandt in the sheet and headed for the door. Birger exited first to make sure the coast was clear. Sverre took hold of Heddy's hand, and Soli followed them outside. The main house looked quiet. Soli locked up, threw the key on the pebbles next to a stone slab, and rushed after the others across the dewy grass. As they started crossing the field, a man shouted from the driveway between the church and the villa. Another one yelled back. A shot was fired.

Soli grabbed Sverre's arm. "I heard two voices." She frantically stretched her neck, checking if they were all there. Suddenly, her heart seemed to stop, and she couldn't breathe. Wide-eyed and with a tremor in her voice, she exhaled, "Where's Nikolai?"

CHAPTER NINETEEN

SOLI SPUN AROUND in the direction of the gunshot. The sound of her heartbeat thrashed in her ears. She pressed a shaking hand over her shivering mouth. *Please, God, don't take my Nikolai. Not yet. Not now.* She was about to bolt in the direction of the skirmish when Sverre put his arm out to stop her.

"Run to the truck."

Sverre sounded serious. He urged Soli forward then grabbed Heddy's hand again. They bolted across the turf while continually turning their heads. What was happening up there? Arvid still carried the painting, and as they reached the vehicle, he handed it to Soli.

"You girls stay here," Sverre said. "Hide in the front with the professor."

"But, Sverre," Soli protested.

He shook his head. "No, we don't know how far Haraldsen will go to protect his *revier*." He turned to Arvid and Birger. "Come on, we'll sneak around the side."

Birger was still breathing hard. "Our detective is up there alone against that man."

Sverre nodded. "Be prepared, boys… Follow me."

They kept their heads low and hurried farther up the field and took cover behind a row of shrubberies where the gravel road opened to the front yard.

Soli crawled back out of the truck. She'd been scared out of her wits so many times before, but what she experienced here was pure terror. Nevertheless, she was not about to propel herself into the corner of the seat like a turtle. Her love was out there. Waiting safely in the car was out of the question.

"Heddy, you can't run much now, and I—"

Her friend stopped her with an understanding nod. "I would have done the same. I'll stay here with the professor and the painting. Go, Soli."

More gunfire echoed in the valley, tearing through the night air as she sprinted back up the field. She could not tell where the shots came from. A car started up, and the engine revved. Shadows of a man being chased by the vehicle moved chaotically before her eyes. But who was driving? Who was in front of the auto…in danger of being run over?

Soli moved closer and hid behind a tree trunk. She shoved her fist in her mouth to block a scream. The car circled around the front drive, the wheels spinning on the gravel. The figure threw himself to the side only seconds before he was run over.

"Arvid!" Soli called out and started toward the skirmish.

Birger came running toward her. "Wait, Soli. Don't."

She stopped and squeezed her hands until they hurt. "I must help."

"Stay here. The detective knows what he's doing. Let him do his job. We don't want you in the line of fire."

"But who's shooting? Does the minister have a pistol, too?"

"Yes, but he's totally outnumbered."

Soli wanted to scream with agony, but only a whimpering whisper escaped her mouth. "He could still hit one of you."

Arvid got back up and ran after the car. Nikolai was on the side, pointing his pistol at the tires. Sverre stood right behind him. They fired once, twice. Haraldsen's car swerved off the road and into the open pasture and came to a standstill. Sverre ran toward the car, yanked open the door, and pointed his pistol at the driver.

In seconds, Arvid seized the shotgun out of Haraldsen's hands and flung the weapon across the field. He dragged Haraldsen out onto the grass. The man must have been thrust forward as the car abruptly halted and hit his head against the steering wheel. It didn't stop him from kicking and struggling to get out of Arvid's strong grip. Nikolai went behind the pastor and pulled the man's hands back-to-back with the thumbs facing up. With a couple of clicks, he locked a set of handcuffs in place.

Haraldsen still resisted, but Nikolai kept his voice firm.

"Stop that. No need to even try. You won't get away."

Haraldsen spat on the ground in front of Sverre. "I have connections, you know. Wait until they hear about this. You and your little band of outlaws will regret coming here tonight."

"I doubt that very much," Sverre said. "Besides, the detective who just handcuffed you is the law."

Haraldsen screamed, "I will tell them—"

"Why don't you save that for the hearing later,"

Nikolai interrupted. "Right now, it's off to the police headquarters for you. Connections or not, dealing with looted artwork is illegal, and you'll have a hard time talking yourself out of the charges, especially with the overwhelming amount of evidence in the church over there."

"You took a painting," the pastor said. "Which one?"

"Well, for now, we took your latest acquisition…the stolen Rembrandt. The truth is, that portrait became your downfall. But rest assured. We'll be back for the remaining artwork later."

Nikolai sent Arvid a quick nod and took him aside. "I need to do this alone. The risk of driving to the police station with all of you is too great. Place Mr. Haraldsen in the back seat of his car. Sverre can help me take him to the arrest at 19 Moller Street."

"But Sverre needs to stay clear of the Gestapo."

"Absolutely, and I'll have him get out of the car before we arrive at the station. I need you and Birger to take Soli, Heddy, and the professor safely back to Oslo. Maybe Heddy should stay in Soli's room in the basement until we find out where Walter is now."

Soli leaned her head on Birger's shoulder and let out a long breath.

"Stay here until they've gone," Birger said. "Nikolai has this. Haraldsen does not need to see your face. You still have your shop and art colleagues to consider."

They watched Nikolai and Sverre leave with the pastor then walked back to the truck.

"It's late," Arvid said, placing his arm around Soli's shoulders. "Let's get you and Heddy safely to your place. Birger and I will then drive the professor home to his wife."

"Poor Mrs. Holst. She's been beyond herself with worry."

Birger grinned. "But isn't it moments like this that make our work worthwhile? Mrs. Holst and the professor will be back together, and we are once again left with the happy, grateful feeling that we've taken part in a good deed."

Soli climbed onto the back of the truck with Birger and stroked his cheek. "Thank you, Birger. I needed to hear that right now."

Arvid handed her the painting. "I thought you might want to hold this."

Soli nodded and carefully settled down with her back to the cabin. On her lap she held the sheet-covered portrait of Claude Beaulieu, Annarosa Ruber's husband. Words could not explain her feelings. A Rembrandt. A precious artwork with perfect brushstrokes. A painting rescued for the surviving member of the Ruber family.

Birger seemed to understand the joy she felt. He simply eased in next to her and smiled.

Heinz Walter rested comfortably in the back of his car, staring at houses and buildings along the road on his way to the airport. His leather bag sat next to him on the seat. Inside was an envelope with a good sum of money—more than he'd ever received for a transaction before. When a young archaeologist had approached him a few days ago, explaining he had information the lieutenant colonel might find interesting, Walter had been intrigued. The young fellow was clever at bargaining, though—maybe Danes had that talent—and had demanded fifteen percent of the earnings if Walter sold the painting. The fellow was definitely not part of any spy network, but he was no greenhorn, either. The young man knew how to make money on information about ancient artifacts they dug up from the ground. For some unknown reason, the fellow knew about Walter's methods of finding artwork and threatened to expose the lieutenant colonel if he didn't pay up. Walter could, of course, have his men get rid of the fellow for good, but instead thought they could do more business together. The idea was exhilarating.

Selling the musketeer portrait was by far the best deal Walter had ever made. There were plenty more paintings in the world. If he could only find a few more pieces like that, he'd be able to retire as a vastly prosperous man in a short while. He leaned back and smiled to himself. Imagine, he'd had a Rembrandt in his possession. Oh well, he'd rather have the money than an old painting on his wall. Hmm...an early retirement...he liked the sound of that.

Walter had left Haraldsen's farm after dinner. A delicate meal of pheasant and a bottle of wine with the art collector had been the perfect way to celebrate their business deal. An odd man, that Haraldsen, almost frenetic when it came to certain art, but they'd enjoyed a good companionship the last five years. Walter had found interesting artwork the pastor paid good money for.

They drove straight to the airport at Fornebu. Oslo would always be there, and he looked forward to spending time in the old mansion on Oscar Street in the future. He groaned. A future? Yes, he still believed in thriving days ahead. Walter could do well in Norway without Adolf Hitler backing him. He was respected there. People feared him.

What about that young woman who worked in the art shop? For some reason, Walter had the notion she was connected to many of the problems he'd encountered. Yes, she was part of the Oslo art world, but why did she show up every time he learned about special and valuable pieces? Better not take any chances. On his next visit to Oslo, he'd have his men pick her up. That Soli Hansen was probably not as innocent as she looked.

"Ready to go home?" he asked his driver as the car came to a full stop.

"*Ja, Herr Obersturmbannführer*. It will be good to see the family again."

Walter pursed his lips and nodded. His sentiments exactly. Coming home to his house in the Berlin suburb, being greeted by his pretty wife, having those three little ones run around his legs...yes, it all sounded nice after a week of hard work. Who knew? With all the money he was going to earn, they might even move to a warmer climate.

The door to the aircraft stood open, and the engine was already running.

"We're ready for takeoff, *Herr Obersturmbannführer*," the co-pilot said as Walter and his two men entered. He secured the door and placed their suitcases in the back.

Walter kept his leather bag close and found a window seat. He rubbed his face and yawned. Such a demanding week, but it had been worth it. Regrettably, Heddy Vengen wouldn't be there when he returned to Oslo again. He would have liked to get to know her better. He grunted and let out an irritated lip trill. Why were the beautiful ones not to be trusted?

"Fasten your seatbelts," the pilot called from the cockpit.

The roar of the engine as the JU 52 tore down the runway and took flight always made Walter's spine tingle. Had he not enjoyed trading art so much, he might have wanted to become an aviator. Too late now. Soon, he'd be living days of leisure instead.

Once the plane had reached the initial altitude, Walter unbuckled the belt, eased back into his seat, and glanced out the window. Had he dozed off for a short while? His neck was stiff from leaning against the pane. They flew above the clouds now, and the northern sky was still light enough to see the fluffy formations resembling mountains of foam. But what was that in the distance? Walter jerked and sat up straight. The aircraft drew nearer, becoming larger and larger. He growled loudly and shouted, "Airplane approaching. Do you see it?"

One of his men answered promptly, *"Ja, Herr Obersturmbannführer.* I'll go and ask the pilot."

Walter plastered his face against the window as the plane changed direction toward them and made a sharp turn behind the JU 52's tail. Was it a Mosquito fighter plane? The English had terrorized the airspace over Germany with those fighters and had probably downed hundreds of Luftwaffe planes in the process.

Walter stared in mute horror, but as rapidly as it had appeared, the plane was out of sight. Could it have been a simple flyby? He'd even offer a prayer of thanks if that were the case. A few seconds went by, but then a horrendous explosion shattered his airplane, ripping the right side to pieces and drawing the air from the cabin like bursting a giant balloon. Unbearable and brutal pressure squeezed his lungs and tore at every limb. The last thing he noticed was being pulled along with his leather bag toward the breach in the fuselage, his precious earnings dotting the sky like huge snowflakes. Then everything went black.

A WEEK LATER—LIBERATION
DAY

TUESDAY, 8 MAY 1945

CHAPTER TWENTY

OSLO, NORWAY

HAND IN HAND, Soli and Nikolai hurried through the streets of Oslo. General Alfred Jodl of the Third Reich had signed an unconditional surrender at the Supreme Headquarters in Reims, France the day before, and news of the German capitulation had immediately spread like a cleansing wildfire across the world. Today, they wanted to celebrate with young and old. The leaders of their own Home Front had sent out a proclamation:

Our fight has been crowned with victory. Norway is once again free. God bless this precious land of our fathers.

Nikolai had already been at work. The German Army who had commandeered the police headquarters at 19 Moller Street had stood down, and the Home Front had instantly taken control.

The liberation fest had already started the evening before. As soon as the German capitulation was announced, people had come out of the woodwork to cele-brate. Now, overcrowded cars drove around with people hanging out of the open windows, some sitting on the roof, rejoicing and waving their hand flags. Young men rode bicycles, cheering. Even the weather showed its best side. Fourteen degrees Celsius was not bad for the first half of May. All over the country, flags were raised. One after another, they fluttered in the spring breeze until the blue and white cross on the red background dotted the land. Everyone wanted to be part of the festivity. Hordes of people crunched together and lined up in the crowd along Karl Johan Street. Their lovely parade street stretched from the pale-yellow royal palace to the Central Station. Young and old danced, cheered, and waved to each other.

It was a different scene now than Soli and Nikolai had witnessed five years earlier. Escorted by Norwegian riding police, dense rows of German soldiers wearing steel helmets and carrying weapons had stomped down the same street. Drummers had marched in front, followed by soldiers playing brass instruments. Only hours later, Hitler's army had infiltrated their country. The following days, thousands more had arrived. It had been a lightning attack without mercy. Oslo had been thrown into a chaos of uncertainty and dictatorship.

Today, fear and bewilderment had been replaced with laughter, happy smiles, and hope.

Nikolai pulled Soli in to stand in front of him, facing the street. "No one knew the war would last so long," he said and wrapped his arms around her waist. "We'll always remember this day. It'll be celebrated every year from now on, I'm certain of it." He kissed her earlobe and whispered. "This is my second favorite day."

She gave him an inquisitive stare.

Nikolai winked. "My very favorite day was when you said yes to marrying me."

She folded her hands around his. "Mine, too." Warmth radiated throughout her body. "It's unbelievable. We're free," she said softly, her face holding a grin that couldn't be contained.

"What's that, my darling?"

Soli lifted her chin and shouted. "We're free!" She turned her head to Nikolai. "I've waited so long to say those words."

Someone grabbed her arm in the crowd. "Hello, sister."

"Sverre. Where's Heddy?"

"Oh, she's coming. She wanted to go by Rolf's first. We thought we'd bring all the boys and drive out to Klemetsrud and visit Far. It's been several years since I last saw him. You two should join us?"

"Absolutely. Far will be thrilled to see you again. He hasn't said so in many words, but he's been both proud and worried about your involvement with the resistance."

"That's why I wanted to bring our men, too. Far should meet the good people we've worked with."

"And Heddy? He doesn't know about you two."

Sverre pulled a lopsided grin. "Oh, he'll love her. How could he not?"

* * *

Far cried when they all showed up on his doorstep. Even Rolf had joined them. They spent the evening in the small living room of Soli and Sverre's childhood home, talking into the night, sharing stories and experiences, both good and bad. And Sverre was right. Heddy immediately found a place in Far's warm heart. When Nikolai invited him to the wedding, their father laughed with joy.

All day, they'd questioned and discussed whether the German troops would surrender without any trouble. Something must have happened, because they met no resistance on their way back to town in the early morning hours. There was no curfew to uphold, and driving through the streets was no longer a nerve-racking ordeal.

As Arvid stopped the truck in front of Soli's shop, they noticed a couple sitting close together on her doorstep.

Soli jumped off the back of the vehicle and ran over to hug the young man.

"Jacob Ruber. What are you doing here?"

"We came across the border as soon as we heard the news."

The others joined them. In one way or the other, each of them had been involved in getting Jacob to Sweden. Heddy had asked Soli to hide the young Jew, Nikolai had prepared papers for him, Rolf had planned the escape, and Birger and Arvid had taken him on a dangerous drive to the Swedish border. Even Sverre had spent time with him in Stockholm. Jacob looked healthier than the last time Soli had seen him. His eyes were no longer hollow and dull but had a determined, goal-oriented look. He used to appear like a man who'd tremble as an aspen leaf in the slightest breeze. Even though his scarred soul no doubt carried the weight of what had happened to his family, there was a certain optimism in his gaze. Could it have something to do with the young woman by his side? What a sweet smile she had. Her long brown hair was parted slightly off-center and fell softly on her navy-blue cape.

"This is Malka...my wife. Her name means queen, and that's what she is to me."

"Welcome, Malka," Heddy said and embraced the young woman. "We're so happy to meet you."

"Thank you." Malka smiled shyly then lowered her eyes.

Birger patted Jacob on his shoulder. "Congratulations, my friend."

"Where did you two meet?" Arvid asked.

Jacob took hold of Malka's hand. "I found people of my faith in Stockholm. Malka was like me, alone and without knowledge if the rest of her deported family had survived or not. We wanted to come to Norway a few weeks ago, but when we heard that Swedish count, Folke Bernadotte, was organizing a convoy of white-painted buses to drive to Germany and rescue Jewish prisoner, we waited to see if there was any news of our kin." He paused for a moment. "Of the hundreds who were deported on German ships, only two or three Norwegian Jews returned on those buses. We haven't given up on seeing our families again, but my heart tells me they're no longer with us."

Sverre stretched. "We all want to spend more time with you, Jacob, but we should probably get some sleep first. Yesterday was a wonderful but long day."

Soli sat down on the steps next to Jacob. "You came here. Do you need a place to sleep?"

He nodded. "Yes, please. Only until we find out what our options are. I'd like to show Malka your room downstairs where I stayed before. Could we—?"

"Of course."

The sun was already rising, casting shadows between tall buildings.

Heddy gave Soli a hug. "We'll take our leave then. Goodnight, everyone...or should I say good morning?"

She climbed up on the back of the truck with Sverre and Rolf while Birger and Arvid sat in the front. Waving cheerfully, they drove off, shouting with joy, "We are free! We are free!"

Nikolai pulled his shoulders back and smiled. "Come on. Let's go see if Soli has anything to eat."

They walked down the alley next to the shop and entered through the back door. Soli didn't have much food on her shelf, but what she had, she was happy to share. Tomorrow morning, she'd slip out early enough to get a few groceries with her ration card. Even if the war was over, it would take a while to fill up the shelves in the grocery stores. Soli warmed a kettle with blackcurrant juice and made a pot of oatmeal porridge with a dash of cinnamon. Her guests eagerly swallowed every spoonful. Obviously, the poor couple hadn't eaten for a while.

Nikolai leaned back on the sofa. "What are your plans now? As you know, our group has been busy rescuing artwork that belongs to your family. We've also been in and out of your uncle's house on Oscar Street."

Jacob finished the last sip and placed his cup on the table. "We're so grateful for all you've sacrificed. You've put yourselves in danger for our inheritance, for our heritage."

"We haven't located any other surviving member of your family...only you," Nikolai said.

Jacob rubbed a hand across his mouth. "I know. Seems like I'm the only one left."

Soli refilled their cups. "We'll do everything we can to help you regain your rights and take over the ownership of your uncle's house. Much of the china, furniture, and other valuable items are spread all over with the wind, but we have dozens of etchings and drawings—many of them quite valuable. You can keep them as an investment or even for personal, nostalgic reasons, or I could sell some for you...to build up your capital. But the four baroque paintings, Jacob—the Caravaggio, the Rubens, and the two Rembrandts—not only are they extremely valuable... they are part of your heritage, being portraits of your ancestors. It's up to you, of course, but if it were me...I don't think I could part with such treasures."

Jacob took hold of his wife's hand. "Malka and I have talked about our future here. We hope to move into my uncle's house eventually. For right now, we need to adjust to our new life together as free Jews. It'll take time, and preconceived opinions are still everywhere. Prejudice doesn't disappear in a day."

Nikolai gave him a friendly pat on the shoulder. "No, I'm sure you're right about that. There might be people who'll need some time adjusting to the denazification. But I believe we'll get there."

"I have a suggestion," Soli said. "In the next while, the National Art Gallery here in Oslo will start gathering all their treasures that have been hidden since 1939. Many of these are kept in the silver mines in Kongsberg along with some of your baroque portraits. The Ruber collection is still not safe from thieves. You need a place to keep the paintings while you adjust to your life here. How about if I discuss the matter with the gallery's curators and arrange for them to—?"

Jacob cut in. "You mean...hand over my family's artwork to the National Gallery?"

"Not to keep...but as a loan. I have no doubt they'd be thrilled to showcase these portraits by famous master artists. Then, when you and Malka feel you're able to take care of the artwork, you can retrieve your family's legacy. I could even ask them to make a special Ruber exhibition, including the etchings I have downstairs."

Jacob turned to Malka. "What are your thoughts?"

She smiled and nodded. "Nikolai...Soli, we're truly in your debt. It sounds like a safe and good plan. We'll teach our future children about their heritage and their ancestors who walked the Earth before them. The artwork will be part of their inheritance and tradition."

Soli smiled. "Imagine, you can visit the gallery, sit down on a bench, and study your art in a safe environment."

"It's a great plan," Nikolai said. "And when you two are ready, we'll see about reinstating the house. It needs some tender care, but Soli and I, along with the rest of our group, can help you."

Jacob pressed a hand to his heart. "Thank you."

Malka stifled a yawn. "Jacob, we need some sleep."

"Of course," Soli said. "You must be tired." She opened the door to the basement. "Jacob, you know where the room is. There are blankets and quilts down there, too."

Malka threw her arms around Soli's neck and gave her a brief hug then followed Jacob down the stairs.

Nikolai walked to the back door. "Believe it or not, we both have to work in a few hours."

"Jacob and Malka will be all right, won't they?" Soli asked and took hold of Nikolai's hands.

"Yes, my sweet. They're young and have already lost so much. What you've done for them will help them connect with their ancestry."

"Will you be celebrating at your office? I mean, the

police force has been under Nazi supervision for so long. Imagine...men from two extremely different camps have worked together under the same roof. How will you combine your efforts now?"

"It might take a while. I spoke briefly with one of my colleagues earlier today. Dozens from the Gestapo are in hiding. We'll join the Milorg Home Front and surround their camp."

"Be careful, Nikolai." She paused. "I suppose you'll be part of several such actions to protect our homes and help people have normal lives again. By the way, what do you think Walter's plans are now? If he still plans on coming back here, I'd like to know."

"He's unpredictable and probably thinks himself superior even though Germany has surrendered the war."

"He should just stay away. He's not welcome here." Soli stepped closer and fiddled with Nikolai's collar. "Jacob said prejudice doesn't disappear in a day. It'll take some time to heal the wounds. We've had one day of freedom, and already I'm impatient about moving the occupying forces out of our country."

Nikolai stood for a moment. His ocean-blue eyes locked with hers. Then he cupped her face in his hands and brushed his mouth against her cheek. When his lips met hers, she kissed him back, tenderly, and with the knowledge that every fiber of her being belonged to him.

He gently pulled away. "I'll see you later today." Then he walked out.

Soli watched him leave. Her heart swelled with grateful thoughts about freedom, friendship, and Nikolai. But it wasn't over yet. What if Walter showed up again? Even if the war had come to an end, he was still a dangerous man.

~ CAPITOLO V ~

LATE AUGUST 1641

THE EARLY BIRDS chirped outside the window as Annarosa packed the last clothes and food into the duffel bag Claude had brought home from one of his journeys to Belgium. A Portuguese sailor in the town of Duffel had sold him the bag made from leftover scraps of coarse fabric used to repair sails on ships. The sailor had claimed they were much sturdier in rough weather than animal skin. Claude and Annarosa had used the bag in rain and storm before and found it quite water-resistant.

Thinking about the missing painting, Annarosa heard her madre's voice in her mind.

"I need you to fulfill my wish. When you have your portrait painted by the great Rembrandt, it must have Caravaggio's signature of light and dark."

Annarosa had rested her head against Madre's chest and had wept like a child. She'd kept her promise. Rembrandt's chiaroscuro technique was much like Caravaggio's.

"Are you ready?" Claude asked. "The ship sets sail in

an hour. We've already waited a week to embark, and if we're late, we'll have to postpone our journey another seven days until the next passage."

"I only have one more thing to do." Annarosa hurried into the parlor and sat down behind the writing desk. In the drawer was the leather-bound ledger, the one that had been with the Ruber family since her grandfather had started writing it in 1573. She pulled it out and laid it on the desk. Smiling, she gently traced her fingers across the gilded edges and the elaborate carved leaves and borders. How proud she had been when her uncle Yoel had asked her to take care of the old book. She opened the brass locket. All the important acquisitions in the Ruber family were written on these pages. Quickly flipping through the documentation about her personal paintings, she stopped where she'd recorded Claude's portrait by Rembrandt.

Claude Beaulieu al servizio di Sua Maestà il Re Luigi XIII di Francia. Ritratto del suo amico Rembrandt, 1637.

How proud she'd been to record Claude's service with the French king and his Rembrandt painting in the family ledger. Annarosa dipped the pen in the ink bottle and wrote in bold letters in the margin next to the previous inscription. *Rubato, 1641.*

Stolen. How she hoped and prayed they'd be able to find the painting and bring it safely home. Meanwhile, Claude had arranged with the militia guard to place someone to protect their house and servants until he and Annarosa returned.

"Annarosa, we need to go, my love." He stood in the doorway, holding the duffel bag and both swords.

"Yes, Claude. I'm coming."

If she wasn't in such a hurry, she would have recorded the thief's name. Perhaps she would add it later, after they came back to Amsterdam. Although, she hoped by then they'd retrieved the painting, and Wolfert's name would not be important anymore. Annarosa placed the ledger back in the drawer and walked into the hall. She kissed a teary-eyed Simona on both cheeks and followed Claude out to the waiting carriage.

* * *

Annarosa was more than anxious to disembark when the ship finally reached the southern part of Norway. The voyage had been rough sailing with wailing winds across the waves and the swaying motion never-ending. Since her stomach had been less than compliant, she'd diverted her thoughts to Simona's tales of white polar bears and snow in the northern countries. But now that she'd arrived, all Annarosa could see was a charming, small town with wooden buildings, green parks, and gardens in full bloom. She could not speak the language, but after making requests at several offices and businesses, Claude found an interpreter who spoke French. Knowing Wolfert was a week ahead of them, they paid the translator to come along as they visited taverns and inns.

"Have you seen a foreigner with black hair partly hanging across one eye? He's in his thirties and usually wears a peasant's hat in a shade of cornflower blue." The interpreter boldly approached both men and women, but even though he seemed to carry on a lengthy conversation with some people, most of them shook their heads.

Outside the fifth tavern, a coachman had news they needed to hear.

"Oh, yes, I remember him," the driver said. "Peculiar type, he was. Carried a wooden tube on a thin rope around his neck and a small pack on his back. That was all. Didn't say much. His destination was farther up the coast."

"How far?" Claude asked.

"Well, it takes three days to reach Larvik, with stops at inns on the way. The man paid his fare and said he'd travel the rest of the journey on foot. When we arrived, I saw him head for the trail going west through the woodland." The driver paused then added, "He seemed tired, perhaps wounded."

Annarosa gave Claude a concerned look. If she'd scratched Wolfert's skin during the skirmish, he'd need ointment for that wound.

"We need to find an apothecary on the way...just in case," she said.

Claude nodded then turned back to the driver and handed him a small amount of silver coins. "Will you take us there? We'll make it well worth your trip and pay the rest when we reach the destination."

The coachman pursed his lip. "How about your translator comes along as my footboy? My boy is not available the next few days, and I need someone to tend the horses and help me with the carriage."

Claude lifted his eyebrows at the translator. "That would be helpful for us, as well, and you'll be fully compensated for your time."

The interpreter nodded and smiled. "I'd be happy to offer my services."

Pleased that both men were willing, Claude and

Annarosa climbed into the carriage with their bag and swords. So far, they'd been able to trail Wolfert's footsteps...but for how much longer? Once they reached Larvik, who could tell which direction he'd gone?

The next days were bumpy but a heap more pleasant than faring at sea. Annarosa's stomach was still misbehaving, and every so often the coachman had to stop the horses for her to step outside for a temporary halt.

"Wolfert must have connections, perhaps buyers," Claude said, staring out the carriage window on the last day. "A lucrative business, but extremely risky. Stealing art by master painters and selling them to collectors is chancy, and if he were arrested..." He released a heavy sigh.

"What would happen to him?" Annarosa asked, hooking her arm around Claude's.

"Well, if he's not flogged and banned from the town, he could end up hanging from a tree or even the gallows. The law does not favor robbers."

She leaned her head on Claude's shoulder. "If it were up to me, Wolfert could take his punishment with a shorter imprisonment. I just want our painting back."

"A trial with a jury will probably decide the outcome, my dearest. First, we must find the man. I'm afraid once we arrive at our destination and follow this trail into the woodland, we'll be as mice on a treadmill, fruitlessly searching for my portrait."

Annarosa closed her eyes and yawned. The trip was more tiresome than she'd expected. "I'm still glad we're trying. We'll abide by the lead we have so far. If it proves a dead end, we could travel to the capital and look up art collectors and men of influence there. The person Wolfert is selling the painting to must be a man of considerable means."

The carriage rolled into a small town and stopped in front of a medieval stone church. Claude stepped out and conversed with the coachman and the interpreter. Annarosa placed a hand on her loosely laced bodice. Certain she was carrying their child she gently rubbed a hand across her belly. The tiredness, being sick to her stomach, the tightness when she dressed herself in the morning. Although impatient to tell her beloved, she decided to wait for the perfect time to share the news.

Claude opened the carriage door, held out his hand, and helped her out. Green hills of endless forest encircled the cove. Quaint white houses with red roofs dotted the coastal landscape surrounded by a rocky shoreline. Smaller rowboats and a larger sailing vessel floated on the twinkling water.

"I've sent our two men to ask around if anyone knows where Wolfert could be headed. The trail the coachman mentioned earlier is up that way through the beech woods. We should examine that route. The thief is ahead of us by seven days, but someone might have seen him or heard something." He swung his arm enthusiastically. "But other than that, look at this place. From what I understand, this town has a thriving timber business and a well-established ironworks. The region is a prosperous community with local landowners and growing businesses."

Closing her eyes, Annarosa inhaled a deep breath. "There's something about this land that feels good to me."

Claude nodded. "I agree. Should we take a room at one of the inns and survey the area? Hopefully, our search will lead us to Wolfert's potential buyer." He caught her staring toward the trail. "My dearest, even if I'd have to pay to get the painting back, I would."

"I know, Claude. We can only do our best, but we should be prepared that your painting might be lost for good."

They spent the next days searching for information and traveling the highway on horseback to neighboring communities. No one had heard about a stranger with a painting. Claude finally hired someone in town to help them hunt for the thief, but two weeks later, that investment ended fruitless, as well. Wolfert had vanished and their precious work of art with him. Annarosa was not bitter, although deeply saddened, as she realized the portrait of her beloved most likely hung on a stranger's wall somewhere. How could a stranger treasure it as much as she did?

One evening, as they sat on a bench overlooking the fiord, picking up the scent of summer and sea, Annarosa took hold of her husband's hand, interlocking her fingers with his.

"Claude, do you know what I've been pondering?"

"Hmm, no. I'd say it's fairly impossible to know what that beautiful mind of yours mulls over."

She ignored his teasing look and continued. "I'd like for us to spend a few more days here, explore the outskirts of the capital, maybe even the countryside. None of us belong in Amsterdam. I'm an Italian Jew, born in Antwerp. You're a French Catholic. Why not find a common ground? We could return to Amsterdam, sell our townhouse, and bring our paintings, the family ledger, and a few belongings. Of course, we need to ask Simona and a couple of the servants if they'd like to join us. Anything else we can purchase anew." She traced her fingers over her stomach. "Imagine having our child grow up here in these beautiful surroundings."

"Our child?" He tenderly held both her hands. "You are certain of this?"

She smiled. "Yes, Claude. You are to be a father."

With a joyful laugh, he stood and lifted her up, twirling her around again and again.

"Careful. This body is more than just me now."

Claude cupped her face in his strong hands and kissed her lips, gently at first, then with deeper emotion as if they shared a soulful communication.

Annarosa slowly opened her eyes and touched his cheek. "What would your king say if we followed such a notion?"

"I would have to speak with him and his advisers. My service for His Majesty has been voluntary on my part. My position as emissary, on the other hand, was a calling he extended to me. I may be able to present an option to fight less and represent more. Perhaps this country needs a French ambassador *en mission spéciale*. That way, I could still take care of King Louis's interests."

"It could be a special mission of cultural exchange, even political and economic tasks. You would do an excellent job, Claude, but would King Louis negotiate such terms with you? Isn't he almighty, so to speak, like a god in his position?"

"Louis is king by the grace of God. Even though he struggles with illness of the mind and body, he has managed—with the aid of Cardinal Richelieu—to position France as a powerful country in Europe. My relationship with His Majesty is satisfactory, but he often has problems concentrating on the affairs of the state. As chief minister,

Richelieu has an ample influence on both foreign and domestic matters, and I may have to present my ideas directly to him."

Annarosa pressed a finger to her smiling lips. "Dare we do this? I don't need much and could set up home in a new place as long as I have you, my paintings, and my family's ledger...and Simona. We could continue our history here."

He pulled her close and leaned his head against hers. Gazing out at two young men fishing from a small boat, children playing on the shore, and dogs running around, Annarosa dreamed of her future with Claude and their own family.

THE WEDDING

CHAPTER TWENTY-ONE

OSLO, NORWAY MAY 1945

SOLI SAT WITH Heddy and the boys on the benches outside Our Savior's Church. Like always, people ran back and forth between home and work, meetings and leisure, their lives spiced with joys and challenges. But the atmosphere was different. Liberation from their oppressors was more than physical freedom from the claws of an enemy. It was an emotional and almost spiritual openness, being able to choose for themselves, and feeling independent.

"Think of all the times we've sneaked through that iron gate and disappeared into the crypt below the church," Soli said.

Birger grinned. "Yes, and we were raided only once."

Heddy bumped his arm. "That was scary enough."

"Do you think they'll give me back my front tooth now that the war is over?" Birger added with a grin.

Arvid hit his forehead. "Oh, Birger. You are incorrigible. But don't ever change, my friend. Your cheerfulness in the most tragic circumstances has gotten us through more rotten days than I care to remember."

Birger pointed to the gate. "Hey, there's our detective."

Nikolai plonked down on the bench next to Soli. "We just received an interesting report at the station this afternoon. They've found the wreckage of a German plane shot down south of here."

They waited in silence. Where was he going with this?

"An enemy plane less is good news, right?" Arvid asked. "When was this?"

"May first."

Soli tapped a finger on the side of her cheek. "That's the same day we found Heddy and the professor...the same day we found the musketeer painting, and you arrested Pastor Haraldsen."

"That's correct."

Soli gasped. "You're saying Walter was on board? Is he dead?"

Nikolai nodded. "The rescue team found no survivors but were able to identify the bodies of five men—the lieutenant colonel, his assistants, and two pilots. They also came across an uncountable amount of paper-money spread over a rather large area."

Tears trickled down Heddy's beautiful face.

Sverre wiped them away. "What's wrong, my darling?"

"Walter could have had a life with his family. Greed consumes people, even whole cities. It starts small, perhaps as an idea. Then it festers, takes root, and swallows your entire being. Nothing else matters. Our choices define who we are and what we will become."

Sverre pulled her closer. "We just have to make sure we don't ever let greed take charge of our lives."

* * *

The next days, Soli checked the churches in Oslo, even the ones in the suburbs. Finding a clergyman without Nazi connections was not easy. She would have said yes to Nikolai anywhere, but deep inside she longed for a traditional but simple and memorable ceremony. Having a pastor who was willing to sell her country, or one who was prejudiced against different nationalities or people with other beliefs, was out of the question.

As she closed the shop after work, the solution popped up in her mind like a lightning bolt from the sky. How about if they traveled to Uvdal and were married in the medieval stave church? The minister there had given the Germans a few history lessons, but other than that, Sigmund and his wife Connie were kind and a wonderful couple.

That same evening, after speaking with Nikolai, Soli hopped on a bus headed for Klemetsrud to discuss the matter with her father.

"Uvdal?" he said, pouring her a cup of tea. "That's up the valley from Kongsberg, isn't it? It would take us half a day to get there...first the bus to Oslo, then two train rides from there."

"I know, but think of it as a vacation, Far. Where have you traveled the last five years? Nowhere. This would give you the chance to experience some of the scenery of our beautiful country. You could observe the fruit trees in full bloom, eat proper farm meals with meat and cheese, and—"

"I thought you just wanted to get married."

"I do." Soli slowed down her tempo. "But what's wrong with creating an unforgettable day up there with our closest friends and family? I know it's out of the way, but please, say you'll join us."

"How could I say no to you, Soli? I'll come with you. It'll be good to go away for a few days. Since my housekeeper and her little boy moved out, it's been awfully lonely."

"I know, and I promise we'll see each other more often now." She blew on the warm tea and took a small sip. "You'll love the people there, Father. The minister is smart and full of interesting stories. And you've met most of my friends already."

"Have you already asked this minister?"

She lowered her head and smiled. "I have."

"And he said he had the time to receive all of us?"

She looked up again. "He did."

"You knew I'd say yes, didn't you?"

Soli threw her arms around his neck. "Yes…thank you, Far."

* * *

On an overcast Friday afternoon, Soli sat on the back of Arvid's truck, holding Nikolai's hand. Heddy and Sverre had surprised them by preparing a comfortable ride to Uvdal. The wagon bed was decorated with birch twigs boasting newly sprung leaves and tied with bows in red, white, and blue. Cozy quilts and blankets were spread on the floor. Heddy had even arranged a picnic basket with food and drink, and Birger had been by his aunt's bakery and had picked up freshly baked breads and pastries. Even with his bad health, Rolf had said he wouldn't miss the wedding for the world. Sverre had carried Rolf's mattress down three flights of stairs and arranged it on the back of the vehicle so their good friend could lie down if he needed to rest.

Pressed into the corner was a suitcase with her mother's wedding gown. Soli had asked Far if she could have it, and he had reverently lifted the dress out from the chest in his living room. It had always been Soli's dream to wear it one day. Some dreams come true, a thought she'd remember forever.

Next to the suitcase was the crate with the Rembrandt painting. Soli had pondered long where to keep the musketeer portrait. The best option was to gather the four paintings in one location until Jacob and Malka were able to preserve their precious art. What better place for now than to hide them in the silver mines of Kongsberg along with the artwork from the National Gallery?

People they passed waved as Arvid drove through the small town of Kongsberg and started up the road through Nume Valley toward Uvdal. They sang every melody they remembered, from nursery rhymes to love songs and hymns. Sverre and Nikolai told mischievous stories from when they were younger, and Birger pulled a row of hilarious jokes. Soli laughed until her stomach hurt. Yes, life was good.

Far sat up front with Nikolai's mother. Soli had only met the woman the evening before but had immediately felt a close connection. Widowed ten years earlier, Mrs. Lange was elegant and charming. Nikolai treated her with respect and tenderness. Soli had always thought that a man's true nature showed through the way he behaved toward his mother—one more thing she could check on the list of good traits for her future husband.

It was early evening by the time they arrived at the parsonage. How different this day was from Soli and

Heddy's visit a few months earlier. They'd sneaked around, hiding from the Gestapo who'd come to speak with the pastor, and there had been a shooting. Soli pushed those memories from her mind. The past was behind them, and they were starting a new chapter. The last years would always be a part of their book of life—they would never forget what they'd learned—but now she chose to look ahead.

Heddy jumped down from the truck, ran across the grass, and flung her arms around Connie. Soli followed close behind.

Auburn curls bounced on Connie's shoulders, complementing the rusty colors of her knitted cardigan.

Heddy pulled one of the curls. "Look at this unruly mop. Your hair is longer than I've ever seen. I love it."

Connie threw her head back and laughed. "Oh, it's good to see you two girls. I've missed you. And this time, I promise no visits from German officers or Nazi leaders. I can't believe all the commotion we put you through last time you were here...blowing up bridges and whatnot."

"No, no, that was not your fault," Soli protested. "We came to you with a valuable painting. That didn't make the situation any easier."

Connie flipped her hand. "That's all over now. Let's live life today. We have so much to plan for tomorrow. Sigmund and I are thrilled you chose to hold the wedding here. Several of our neighbors have offered a bed or two for our visitors, and you'll eat your meals here with us. Oh, this will be fun." Connie hooked her arms around Heddy's and Soli's and pulled them toward the truck. "Come, introduce me to everyone. I see my Sigmund is already there."

Soli lifted the crate with the Rembrandt from the

truck. "Can you keep this somewhere safe until we can take it to the silver mines?"

"Let's take it inside. I told Thor Hammer about the painting," Connie said.

"That's good. I'd like to preserve this last portrait with the art from the National Gallery until the curators return their collection to Oslo. I'll talk with Thor about placing it with the Ruber paintings we already have there... He is coming, isn't he?"

"Oh, yes, he'll be here for the wedding tomorrow. He wouldn't miss a party with friends."

Heddy helped Soli carry the crate inside and upstairs to the main bedroom where they placed it on the bed.

Connie pushed her curls back. "The painting will be safe here. I can be in the middle of a dream and still hear a pin drop to the floor. Besides, you'll all be here at the parsonage during the day, also."

"Do you want to see it?" Soli asked.

"I'd love to. Let me get some tools to pry open the small tacks and nails along the edge." Connie hurried out. She returned a moment later, carrying a pair of pliers and a hammer.

"The truth is, I asked because I'm dying to see it again before it's packed away for a while."

Heddy squeezed her arms around her stomach. "All the struggles we've had with Walter, my father, and other Nazis because of these paintings. It hasn't been easy."

"No, it hasn't, and I'm so sorry about what you've been through," Connie said, pulling her eyebrows down.

Heddy hooked her arm around Soli's. "We've all had to face hardship and pain, but if I had to choose sides once more, I'd fight for our country again and again."

"I'm with you," Connie said resolutely. "I'm proud of what we've accomplished together."

Soli pulled out every nail and carefully lifted the lid. She drew aside the cloth and revealed the painting.

Heddy sat down on the bed next to the crate.

"Meet Monsieur Claude Beaulieu," Soli announced. "Annarosa Ruber's husband and friend to Rembrandt who painted this."

Connie moved closer. "A Frenchman. He looks like a musketeer. Do you think he taught his wife how to handle a sword?"

"Perhaps."

"He's awfully handsome." Connie put the back of her hand on her forehead, pretending to swoon over the man.

Heddy slapped her shoulder. "Silly...but I do agree with you." She picked up the lid to the crate. "We should probably put this back in place. We have a wedding to prepare."

They folded the cloth on top of the painting, replaced the lid, and gently fastened the nails and tacks to the edges of the crate.

Connie slid the box under the bed. "Soli, why don't you take a walk with Nikolai? Heddy and I will get dinner ready."

Soli smiled and hurried downstairs. She slipped on her shoes in the hallway and went outside. Nikolai was standing with Sigmund next to the stone wall by the road, rubbing his chin and nodding. The pastor was eagerly explaining something, using facial expressions and hands to tell the story.

Sigmund acknowledged her but continued. "So, they used a horse and wagon to move the largest rocks from the field over there to build this wall. Four strong men it took." He held up four fingers. "Four musclemen to lift the heaviest ones. They'd already dug the ditch and parked the loaded wagon about here. Huffing and groaning, they carried the first stone, placed it in the ground, and went back to pick up another. But when they returned, a rather sturdy billy goat with horns as long as an arm and a beard that hung down to its cloven hooves stood on the wagon. The animal scowled at the men and stomped his foot on the wagon floor, blowing steam out of his nose and mouth like a bull. The four workers turned and ran as they fast as they could, hiding behind the stone wall. Heaving for breath, they popped their pale faces above the wall. The triumphant billy goat lifted his head high and with a gloating look on his face, scanned the area before he hopped down and quietly trotted away.

Nikolai burst out laughing. "My guess is that those men didn't tell this story."

"Oh, no, no. How could they? What an embarrassment to their manliness. The minister's wife who'd hired them stood in the doorway watching the whole scene. She kept a journal during the time her husband served here. It must have been around the turn of the century. I found her diary among the old books on the shelves in the living room when Connie and I moved here. The woman had a sense of humor and wrote down everyday tales with absurdity and her comical viewpoint. You should read it sometime. It's quite entertaining."

Sigmund touched Soli's arm. "But now, dear Soli, I'll let you have your man. I'll see if Connie needs some help with dinner preparation."

Nikolai took hold of Soli's hand. "Sigmund is full of stories."

"Yes, he has an inexhaustible repertoire of both historical facts and funny anecdotes from the area. I could listen to him for hours."

They strolled toward the church. A brisk, dancing wind swept across the lawn between the main house and the stave church. To marry Nikolai in such an old building was another dream come true. The wooden structure had stood there for centuries, the middle section dating all the way back to the year 1168.

"I know that look," Nikolai said. "There's more than our wedding on your mind right now. You're excited about this old church, the history...this whole place."

"But, Nikolai, look at that house of worship. How many people have been married there before us, do you think? Couples like us, in love and with hopes for the future. Isn't it amazing? I imagine a line of brides from different time periods walking up those stairs and entering that heavy, tar-stained door. The first one is donned in a woolen tunic with a trailing hem. Her gown has long, open sleeves, and she wears a flat veiled cap on her head. The next one wears a dress with a high waistline and skirts gathered at the front. Her long hair is rolled up inside a mesh headdress with a padded roll on top. Then comes the bride from Henry VIII's era. She carries a gabled hood on her head, and her gown flaunts huge cuffs trimmed with ermine and a brocade skirt with gold embroidery."

"I take it she wasn't a farmer's maid," Nikolai said with a smile.

"No, she was part of the aristocracy before one of the kings removed her title."

"Good to know." Nikolai still snickered. "Go on, Soli. Who else is in this line-up?"

"Hmm...I believe next up is a woman who looks like

Annarosa Ruber and her mother Fabiola from the baroque paintings we've found. You've seen both their portraits."

"Is this bride carrying a sword?"

Soli slapped his arm and laughed. "You just can't help yourself, can you? You're thinking about Annarosa who chose to have her portrait done with her weapon across her lap. No, Nikolai, this bride is not carrying her sword when she's about to give her marriage vows." Soli pulled her shoulders back. "Where was I? Yes, the baroque bride wears an enormous gown with petticoats, padded rolls and huge, puffed sleeves with double, lace-edged cuffs. In fact, she loves lace, pearls, and feathers."

"Sounds like quite a chore to get dressed," Nikolai said.

A whistling sound shot across the yard. Sverre called out, "Dinnertime."

"We should go back," Nikolai said. "How about we rush forward to Soli, the bride of 1945? What will she be wearing tomorrow?"

"Very sneaky, Nikolai. You'll have to wait and see."

CHAPTER TWENTY-TWO

THE NEXT DAY, the breeze had calmed. Birds were chirping in the trees on the hill. Even the crooked iron crosses behind the stave church had a certain charm in the morning sun, and dew on the grass seemed to fade before their eyes.

Connie and Heddy had chased the men outside after breakfast, claiming the house was off limits to menfolk, especially if they were a detective.

A long mirror stood propped up against a chair in the living room. Mor's wedding gown was a perfect fit. Soli adored the sheer chiffon sleeves and the matching ruffle that softly flowed around the neckline. A broad silk band had a dozen pearl-like buttons on the back, and two layers of tulle covered the satin skirt.

Connie peered out the kitchen window. "Thor's here... on his motorcycle."

Soli rushed over. He came. Thor had been a pillar of strength for the local community in Uvdal, fighting the enemy with a group of men led by Connie. Eager to go outside, Soli started toward the door.

Heddy pulled her back. "Oh, no, you. Let's finish your hair first. You can talk with Thor about the painting later. Besides, he's on his way to the church now."

A bit embarrassed, Soli obediently sat down on a stool in front of the mirror. Connie teased the top of Soli's hair and carefully brushed it back. She added a few pins but left the wavy length in the back. Heddy attached Mor's bridal veil fringed with lace. The sheer fabric draped Soli's shoulders and hung all the way to the floor. Then Connie added a simple floral wreath of daisies and lilacs to crown Soli's head.

"Now, stand up," Heddy said and handed Soli the wedding bouquet with flowers like the ones in the wreath.

Soli closed her eyes. The sweet scent had the promise of an approaching summer of warmth and long, light days.

"I'm ready," she said.

They walked out. Heddy and Connie went first, both carrying a twig of lilac in their hands.

Then followed Soli.

Father stepped forward and offered his arm. "You look lovely, my girl. I wish your mother could be here."

"She's here, Far. I feel it."

As they turned to walk the path to the church, a car came up the dirt road and drove into the parking lot outside the fence. The doors opened, and out came Professor Holst and his dear wife, and from the back seat, Jacob and Malka.

Soli glanced at Heddy. "Did you invite them?"

She nodded.

Soli placed her palm on her chest. "Oh...I'm so happy to have them here. I was afraid the trip would be too strenuous for the professor, so I never mentioned the wedding. And Jacob and Malka told me they were going out of town."

"Oh, they just said that to surprise you. They were actually coming here."

Soli handed Heddy the bouquet, lifted her skirt, and hurried toward the guests. She hugged each one. "You've made me so happy. Thank you."

The professor's wife touched Soli's hair and the sleeves on her gown. "You look absolutely beautiful, my dear."

"Thank you, Mrs. Holst. This dress belonged to my mother."

Soli hooked her arm around Jacob's wife and started back to the others. "How are you, Malka?" she asked low.

"Better with every day. But even though I wish to release all the sad memories, I realize it'll take a while."

"The scars won't go away completely. They'll be a part of you. But with time, the wounds will heal. And with Jacob by your side, you can choose to raise yourself above the heart-rending losses you've experienced. I lost my mother during the first summer of the war. I've cried because I wanted her here for our wedding. But somehow, today, I feel she's with us. That's a great comfort for me."

"I know we have a wedding now, but I just wondered...do you know if someone in Jacob's family had an ancestral record...like a family tree or a document describing their genealogy? One day, when we have children of our own, I'd like to teach them where they came from."

"Well, we haven't found a complete record, but I have an old ledger that belongs to Jacob now. It's a journal that one of his forefathers started in 1573. When you're settled, I will give that to you. Several generations are recorded on the first pages, starting with Isaac Ruber of Malta. The Rubers came to Norway around 1641, and we can try to find their descendants in the national archives. These old church books, census records, and more have been safely kept in the silver mines in Kongsberg during the war, but once those archives are back in Oslo, we should be able to do some research and trace the lineage up to Jacob today."

"Will you help us?" Malka's voice cracked with emotion.

"Of course. Just give it some time. I'm not sure when they'll open the archives for the public. It may take a while."

"Thank you." Malka smiled and squeezed Soli's hand. "I'm so glad we can be here to share your special day."

"We're almost like family now."

"Are you ready?" Heddy handed Soli the bouquet and adjusted the veil.

"Yes, everything is fine. Can you ask our guests to go ahead to the church?"

With Professor Holst and the rest of the last visitors well on their way, Soli accepted Far's arm, and they followed Connie and Heddy, treading slowly the path that rose to the church stairs. As they entered the heavy wooden door, the shining timbre of a tenor voice sounded from the organ gallery above.

"Our Birger," Heddy said low.

Soli narrowed her brows and whispered back, "He sings? It sounds beautiful."

Birger's rendition of *Now the Woods Awaken* seemed just right for the times they were in. Far led Soli slowly up the aisle and presented her to Nikolai. She wasn't nervous...

well, perhaps a couple of whimsical butterflies danced in her stomach...but mostly, a feeling of contented joy filled her being. Nikolai held both her hands while they listened to Birger finishing the fifth verse. Far found a seat next to Mrs. Lange, and Sigmund stepped forward. The minister spoke of friendship, loyalty, and trust. He explained how their days were filled with choices and why we choose to love. He closed with the words: *Once we've chosen true love, we need to love our choice.*

Sverre presented the rings, and when Nikolai and Soli proclaimed the solemn vows, tears of joy ran down her face. As Nikolai tenderly kissed her, the church bells started ringing, and everyone clapped. Was it possible to feel such joy? She would wrap up this memory and keep it in her heart forever.

The bells kept chiming. Soli turned and asked, "Who's pulling the rope in the bell tower?"

Sverre grinned. "Arvid. He's always wanted to try, and now he had the opportunity. I hope he finishes soon. It's quite loud."

The heavy clanging of loud metal bells continued. When silence finally returned to the chapel, Soli exhaled a breath of relief and smiled, and a very content-looking Arvid came down the gallery stairs and joined them.

"That was fun," he said. "Anybody else want to get married so I can do it again?"

Laughter filled the chapel, the kind that shares the space like a gift among close friends.

Nikolai grabbed Soli's hand and walked her down the aisle and outside into the sunshine. She floated on air as the silken skirt swooshed with every step, passing by smiling, friendly faces who only wanted their happiness. While Connie directed the guests to help set up a long table in the garden, Rolf took photographs of the newly married couple. By the time they'd posed next to the altar, in front of the stave church, and between the blossoming trees, Sigmund rang the dinner bell.

"Let's have the newlyweds there in the middle of the table with Nikolai's mother and Soli's father on either side," Sigmund suggested. "The bride and groom have asked for an informal setting, but if any of you want to say a few words throughout the evening, please let me know." He put his hands out. "Thanks to my Connie, willing neighbors, and all of you, we'll partake of a feast today. Sit, enjoy, and as they say in France...*bon appetit!*"

The table looked lovely with ivory linen tablecloths, pale-yellow china, and cobalt goblets. Serving trays with cured meats and sausages, baked trout, potato salad, kohlrabi puree, and pickled vegetables were placed down the middle. On a small side table were cloudberries with whipped cream and cakes for dessert. Sigmund said grace, thanking their Maker for the abundant blessings they enjoyed. Throughout the feast, the sound of a spoon clinking against glass brought the chat and discussions to temporary stillness as the guest stood to propose a toast or say a few kind words about the loving bond of matrimony.

After the meal, Soli spoke with Thor on the lawn as Arvid and Birger sauntered toward them.

"We still need to get the Rembrandt to safety," Soli said. "Any thief would be glad to get their hands on such a treasure."

"We'll go with Thor," Arvid said. "We wouldn't want the newlyweds to spend their special day on the back of a dusty truck."

Soli protested, "But I should—"

"No 'buts'. The silver mine is only a ninety-minute drive from here. We'll be back before you know it."

Birger smiled at Soli. "Will you promise me a dance later?"

"Of course. I'll look forward to it."

As they left, Nikolai put his arm around Soli's shoulders. "Satisfied?"

"Yes, it's always a feeling of melancholy and sadness when I give up a painting...as if I mourn the parting." She gazed up at him. "But we'll see it again soon. And besides, I have you, don't I? That's pretty good, too."

"It had better be." He glanced toward the cemetery on the hill. "Heddy's up there by her father's grave with your brother. It can't be easy for her. Their father-daughter relationship was quite strained."

"It was, but I believe she's learning to forgive him."

Soli's glance swept around the lawn and garden. Where was the professor? She'd promised to tell him about the musketeer painting. Now might be a good time to explain the story about the four baroque portraits and their former owners.

"Who are you looking for?" Nikolai asked.

"Professor Holst."

He pointed to the stairs by the stave church. "Up there with his wife."

"Good. I need to have a chat with him. Why don't you mingle with our other guests while I sit down with the professor? He deserves a proper explanation as to why Walter locked him up."

*

As evening approached and shadows from the trees danced on the stone wall, Connie hung lanterns from the branches. One of the neighbors came by, carrying his accordion. He pulled out a chair and started playing well-known songs, many they hadn't heard for years. Father sat at the table, talking with Mrs. Lange. Jacob and Malka stood by the grassy hill, her head on his shoulder, watching the valley down below and the mountains fading in the distance.

Nikolai came up and grabbed Soli around the waist. "Dance with me, wife! The musician is playing a waltz."

"My, you've become strict since we said our vows."

He laughed, swung her around, and pulled her into a close position. Gracefully, Nikolai swept her into the three-step. Slow, quick, quick. Slow, quick, quick. Waltzing on the grass was a seldom affair, not very elegant, and their feet were not in perfect sync. But Soli didn't mind. When the musician changed to a modern swing tune, the whole party came out on the grounds. Even Father stepped in beat to the rhythm, smoothly following Mrs. Lange's willowy movements. Goodbye to German songs. No more restrictions. Spontaneously, Soli kicked off her shoes and danced as she never had before—around and around in circles—twirling as Nikolai spun her under his arm.

As the truck returned, Soli stopped dancing and glanced over Nikolai's shoulder.

"They're back. Imagine...centuries after it was stolen, the Rembrandt musketeer painting is once again reunited with the rest of the Ruber collection."

A warm, grateful feeling filled Soli. Soon, she'd meet with the curators and discuss a special exhibition in the National Gallery.

She let go of Nikolai's hand and started walking toward the boys.

"Where are you going, wife?" Nikolai said, laughing.

"I promised Birger a dance."

"Go ahead. I'll twirl my mother."

Soli walked up to Birger, curtsied, and held out her hands. He spun her into a tango position first then led her fluidly around the table, dipping her now and then, and striding forward cheek to cheek with fervor. She laughed when he ended by supporting his arms around her waist while she arched backward.

Soli held a hand on her heaving chest. "Oh, let me catch my breath. You can do more than sing, young man. You move well, too."

Birger bowed his head and chuckled. Who knew their cheerful friend had so many talents?

"I want to thank you for your contribution in the church earlier. Where did you learn to sing like that?" Soli asked.

"I come from a musical family. My mother played the piano, and Pa improvised on guitar. When they noticed how much I enjoyed singing, they had me audition for a boys' choir. I spent my growing up years with that choral group."

"I had no idea."

"Well, we've been busy with other things, haven't we? Chasing the enemy, rescuing artwork, and such. My singing hasn't been prioritized for a long while."

"But you'll pick it up again now?"

"Yes, I'd like to study music, maybe give voice lessons. The ultimate goal is to direct a choir."

"You're always full of surprises, Birger."

"What is he full of?" Arvid walked up with a teasing look on his face.

"We were just talking about Birger's future plans," Soli said. "How about you, Arvid? What will you do now?"

239

He cleared his throat. "I've spoken with Nikolai. I'd like to continue catching bad people, and he's looking into what I need to pursue a career as a detective."

Soli grabbed the men and pulled them in for a hug. "Come here...I'm so proud of you both."

"Working with you has been a pleasure," Arvid said.

"I feel the same way, Arvid."

Soli sat down on a bench under a birch tree, watching everyone. It was more than the wedding. The freedom they'd longed for had finally arrived. Their country was still out of order, but they were all healing. One day, their land would recover, as well. As she sat there contemplating what lay ahead, Thor came and sat next to her.

"You'll have to come visit soon. Remember, I have your four paintings."

"You know they're not mine to keep...although, that would be a dream."

She pointed toward Jacob and Malka. The couple was still dancing.

"You met those two today, didn't you? That young man is the only one left of the Jewish Ruber family in Oslo. He is the sole descendant to their estate, and the paintings belong to them now. My plan is to ask the National Gallery to take care of the four baroque portraits for the time being...until things settle down."

"That sounds like a sensible plan."

"I want to come back here and go with you to the silver mines when the curators pick up all their own crates. I'm sure they'll be happy to have such treasures on display in the National Gallery until Jacob can take care of them himself."

Nikolai plunked down next to them on the bench. "So,

my friend, what will you be doing now that you're done chasing the enemy?"

Thor lifted his eyebrows. "Me? I'll be fishing all summer. I'll go up to that old Milorg cabin you and I skied to last winter. Think I'll spend some days there, clean out some of the old tins with stale crackers...you know, just do as little as possible until I start working for the Home Guard. They've offered me a job I can't refuse."

"Congratulations," Soli said. "It all sounds great... except from the stale crackers. We might even come visit."

"Please do. It's a nice place to stay when we don't have to worry about hiding from the Germans."

Nikolai nudged Soli's shoulder. "Now, wife. What would you like to do?"

"Well, a vacation sounds nice. Other than that, I'll be busy for years to come, trying to track down looted art. There are more paintings out there that need to be returned to their rightful owners."

"You're bound to get into trouble again, you know that?" Nikolai winked at her.

"No doubt, and some may not want to part with artwork they've stolen or hidden. At least, we won't have to fight Hitler and his soldiers." She smiled coyly. "I'll need some friends and a handsome detective to help me out."

"I'll always be here," Nikolai said.

"So will we." Sverre came up with his arm around Heddy's waist.

Birger and Arvid followed them. Rolf came last, leaning heavily on his cane.

"Come sit here." Nikolai stood and helped Rolf down on the bench.

"So, wife. I have a surprise for you," Nikolai said.

"We're already here in this beautiful scenery, and Connie has two bicycles, sleeping bags, and a tent we can borrow. How about a honeymoon? We'll ride farther up the valley for a few days, camp by a river, and listen to birds singing. We might even visit Thor at the Milorg cabin and eat fried fish and stale crackers."

"But my art shop. My customers?"

Sverre laughed. "Come on, little sister. How can you refuse such an offer?"

"We took the liberty of hanging up a sign on your display window before we left," Birger said, grinning.

Soli shot glances at everyone there. What were they up to now? She folded her arms. "A sign, huh? What does it say?"

The same thing that many of the shopkeepers have written on their doors lately:

Closed due to joy.

AUTHOR'S NOTE

Closed due to joy.

Isn't that beautiful? And true, as well. Already, on the evening of 7 May 1945, the news of peace reached every corner of the land. People who lived then refer to the feeling they had as indescribable. Peace, at last. They'd waited so long. The day after, grown-ups didn't go to work, children skipped school, and stores were closed due to joy. Happy shouts and chants like, "The victory is ours. The victory is ours. We have won. The victory is ours," rang through the streets. People tore down their black-out curtains and threw them on one of the many bonfires.

Milorg, the military resistance organization, also called "the boys in the woods", consisted of about forty thousand men and women, many of them teenagers. When the Germans surrendered in May 1945, *Milorg* were given the responsibility to aid in an orderly and quiet transition from war to peace. They kept guard, helped arrest Norwegian Nazi-supporters, informants, and others who were suspected of treason or torture.

The Norwegian novelist Vera Henriksen (1927-2016) —who'd been recruited into XU, a branch of the resistance—wrote about *the Victory in Europe Day* several decades after the war, "I was eighteen and behaved like a giddy eighteen-year-old—and at the same time, it felt as if I were a hundred."

Toward the end of the novel, Jacob Ruber mentions the convoy of white buses organized by Swedish count Folke Bernadotte already before the war had ended. To avoid attacks, the buses were painted white and had the Red Cross emblem and a Swedish flag painted on every side and even on the roof. Close to twenty thousand Norwegians, Danes, and a few other nationalities were evacuated from the Nazi concentration camps around Europe. After the war, more than ten thousand more were brought home. Of the thirty Norwegian Jews who survived the camps, two or three were brought back on the buses.

White Buses to Auschwitz is a Norwegian organization that arranges school trips to former concentration camps today. From the upstart in 1992, thousands of young people have learned about human worth and human rights, democracy, and how to stand up for what's good. The organization also arranges trips for adults.

Oslo or Christiania—what is the name of the Norwegian capital?

Soli and her friends are always running around Oslo. But why does the thief Wolfert call the capital Christiania? From the year 1000, the town was called Oslo. But when Christian IV—the king of Denmark and Norway—rebuilt the town after a horrible fire in 1624, he renamed it Christiania.

For those of my readers who have started another of

my series called the Mysteries of the Modern Ladies Society, you will see that the name of the capital is spelled Kristiania. The difference in the spelling came in 1877 and remained such until the name was changed back to Oslo in 1925. A bit confusing, but I hope it will clarify the name for those who are interested in the small details.

I'd like to add a few words about the wonderful Rembrandt van Rijn. What an artist he was, but his life was not an easy one. He adored his wife Saskia, and the many drawings and paintings of her verify that. They met the way Saskia explains to Annarosa, and I've described their home as accurately as possible.

Their children were christened in Dutch Reformed churches in Amsterdam. The first son was named Rumbertus after Saskia's father. The infant died soon after birth. Then followed two daughters, both christened Cornelia after Rembrandt's mother. Each of them also died after a few days. They called their fourth child Titus van Rijn. He was born in 1641 and survived his father. Unfortunately, the boy saw little of his mother. Saskia died from either tuberculosis or consumption when Titus was only nine months old. In Brushstrokes from the Past, she is pregnant with Titus but far from healthy. Rembrandt confides his worries to Annarosa and is genuinely afraid of losing Saskia.

Another fun fact is when we first meet Professor Holst, he enthusiastically describes different places archaeologists dig for hidden artifacts. He has the idea that glacier archaeology would be interesting, but the work of systematically gathering finds from the glaciers did not come until sixty-two years later. The mountains of Norway have been a vital hub of these discoveries. Because of global warming, these ice patches have an uncertain future. Archaeologists are well aware of the emergency.

The Viking period covers the years 800 to 1050 when Scandinavians traveled to other parts of the world. The professor mentions working on the dig for the Oseberg ship in 1904. The richly decorated ship was part of a burial site for the two women onboard. He also describes the finds of a woman from the Iron Age and a man who was nine thousand years old. I've connected Holst to several of these amazing archaeological finds to show his expertise and to explain how it was possible for Wolfert's skeleton and belongings to be unearthed three hundred and four years later.

With this fourth book in *the Soli Hansen Mysteries*, WWII has finally come to an end. The dual timeline series follows three baroque painters—Caravaggio, Rubens, and Rembrandt— and the art technique chiaroscuro has been prevalent in a different painting in each novel. Two stories have also continued in all four books. Each novel can be read as a standalone, but they are more enjoyable when read in order, as both the WWII story and the account from the seventeenth century progress. I loved writing *Of Darkness and Light*, *The Other Cipher*, *Hidden Masterpiece*, and *Brushstrokes from the Past* and hope you'll enjoy the journey.

ABOUT THE AUTHOR

HEIDI ELJARBO grew up in a home full of books, artwork, and happy creativity. She is the author of award-winning historical novels about courage, hope, mystery, adventure, and romance in the midst of challenging times.

After living in Canada, six US states, Japan, Switzerland, and Austria, Heidi now calls Norway home. She lives with her husband on a charming island and enjoys walking their Wheaten Terrier in any kind of weather, hugging her grand-children, and has a passion for art and history.

Her family's chosen retreat is a mountain cabin, where they hike in the summer and ski the vast white terrain during winter.

Heidi's favorites are her family, God's beautiful nature, and the word *whimsical*.

You can find more information about Heidi and her books at

https://www.heidieljarbo.com

PLEASE LEAVE A REVIEW

Thank you for reading *Brushstrokes from the past*.
Reviews mean the world to an author. Please consider
leaving one for this book on your favorite store.
These reviews are greatly appreciated.

Made in the USA
Las Vegas, NV
19 September 2022

55615621R00152